REVVER
THE SPEEDWAY SQUIRREL

THE BIG RACE HOME

Also by Sherri Duskey Rinker

Revver the Speedway Squirrel

REVVER
THE SPEEDWAY SQUIRREL
THE BIG RACE HOME

Sherri Duskey Rinker

ILLUSTRATED BY **Alex Willan**

BLOOMSBURY
CHILDREN'S BOOKS
NEW YORK LONDON OXFORD NEW DELHI SYDNEY

BLOOMSBURY CHILDREN'S BOOKS
Bloomsbury Publishing Inc., part of Bloomsbury Publishing Plc
1385 Broadway, New York, NY 10018

BLOOMSBURY, BLOOMSBURY CHILDREN'S BOOKS, and the Diana logo
are trademarks of Bloomsbury Publishing Plc

First published in the United States of America in October 2021
by Bloomsbury Children's Books

Bloomsbury books may be purchased for business or promotional use. For
information on bulk purchases please contact Macmillan Corporate and Premium
Sales Department at specialmarkets@macmillan.com

Library of Congress Cataloging-in-Publication Data
Names: Rinker, Sherri Duskey, author. | Willan, Alex, illustrator.
Title: Revver the speedway squirrel : the big race home / by Sherri Duskey Rinker ;
illustrated by Alex Willan.
Other titles: Big race home
Description: New York : Bloomsbury Children's Books, [2021] |
Series: Revver the speedway squirrel
Summary: Revver the squirrel is now an accepted part of the race team (more or
less), but he still has a lot to learn, and when the team travels to the airport for a
distant race, Revver wanders into the terminal looking for his friends, and gets lost.
Identifiers: LCCN 2021018102 (print) | LCCN 2021018103 (e-book)
ISBN 978-1-5476-0367-1 (hardcover) • ISBN 978-1-5476-0368-8 (e-book)
Subjects: LCSH: Squirrels—Juvenile fiction. | Automobile racing—Juvenile fiction. |
Pit crews—Juvenile fiction. | CYAC: Squirrels—Fiction. |
Automobile racing—Fiction. | Pit crews—Fiction. | Lost children—Fiction.
Classification: LCC PZ7.R476 Rh 2021 (print) |
LCC PZ7.R476 (e-book) | DDC 813.6 [Fic]—dc23
LC record available at https://lccn.loc.gov/2021018102

Book design by Jeanette Levy
Typeset by Westchester Publishing Services
Printed and bound in the U.S.A.
2 4 6 8 10 9 7 5 3 1

To find out more about our authors and books visit www.bloomsbury.com
and sign up for our newsletters.

1

Zoom! Zoom! Zoom! Zoom! Zoom! A pack of cars raced by in a blur. They were moving so fast and *so close together* that Revver had trouble telling them apart.

Revver looked on from pit road, where all the racing teams waited and watched. Many crew members wore headphones, listening for information from the drivers on their radios. Revver stood with the rest of his team, ready to jump into action when their team driver, Casey, needed to make a pit stop.

Forty cars had started the race. Casey's car was still grouped in with the lead cars. Revver counted.

Their car was fifth. Two hundred laps down, sixty laps to go. *Yesssss! Come on, Casey!* Revver cheered him on.

Yesterday, Revver and Jeff, one of the mechanics, had worked together on a setup change—adjusting the shocks—to help the car handle better for the driver. It was a perfect job for Revver: he was just the right size to get inside the wheel well! So far, that little change was paying off. Their car was running perfectly!

Revver got a few pats on the back and some compliments from the crew during the race. Susan smiled and said, "Nice job," and Trevor, giving him a quick ear rub, said, "It's lookin' good out there, Rev." Even Jack, the grumpy team owner, gave Revver a smile and a little nod (which was as close to being nice as Jack ever got).

But the race was not over yet, and anything could happen. Just like the cars, Revver's thoughts were racing. He took a deep breath to try to calm the butterflies in his stomach as he strained to watch from atop Jeff's shoulder.

Then Revver heard a squeal and then **BANG-***bang. Bang!*

*Oh no! **A crash!*** Two cars hit the wall and spun across the track. Soon, other cars got tangled up in the mess, crashing and spinning.

The team could not see what had happened. Everyone held their breath, listening to the radio.

They heard the spotter say, "Watch it, Casey—Dwayne's spinning out to your left."

"Gotcha. I see it," the team heard Casey say.

Silence.

Then they heard the spotter yell, "You're clear! Go, go, *go*!"

"That was close!" Casey's voice rang out.

With lightning-fast reflexes, Casey drove through the mash of crashing cars without any damage. The team cheered! Revver felt himself breathe again.

Casey's voice came onto the radio again. "I gotta thank Jeff and Revver for the suspension work. It's handling awesome. Nice job, guys."

The flagger waved the yellow flag: caution. Casey was coming in for a pit stop, and the team stood ready.

When Casey stopped, everyone, including Revver, jumped over the wall. Revver watched from the ground but stood out of the way. Someone added fuel to the car. The windshield and the nose of the car were brushed off. The jackman lifted the car. Bill and the other tire changer jumped to action. Revver carefully watched everything. He was always trying to learn and was always ready to help.

When Bill took out the second tire, something caught Revver's eye. Standing one foot tall, he was the perfect height to see it: under the wheel well, something did not look right.

Everything was moving so fast. Revver acted quickly. He ROARED over the noise of the engine, **"Vr-vr-vr-VRRROOOOM!"** and he jumped under the car.

The entire team stopped, shocked. All eyes were on Revver. Valuable seconds ticked by.

Revver was *under* and *behind* the wheel. Bill squatted down, squinting, to watch. He saw Revver press a loose spring rubber back in, securing it. In a blink, Revver jumped out—and out of the way. The jack dropped, and Casey roared back to the race.

Everyone exhaled in relief.

"What happened?!" Casey radioed out.

"Loose spring rubber. Revver caught it."

"Right on, Revver!"

Casey rolled back onto the track. He was in third place now. The green flag waved. The race started again.

Bill gave Revver a quick rub behind the ears. "I'm proud of ya, buddy." Nothing made Revver as happy as making Bill happy.

Sometimes, being small meant that he was especially good at finding big problems. There were advantages to being the only squirrel on the team.

2

Casey had finished a solid second place. It was a good day.

As the team packed up, Revver paused for a moment while he waited for his next instructions. He glanced down and noticed the orange braided cord tied around his ankle. And for the first time in a while, he thought of his sister, Sprite. She had made the chain for him. He sighed. It had been a long time since he'd left home and joined the race team. There had been many tracks and many races since then. He loved his life at the tracks, around Bill and the team, and the cars. But sometimes, when he thought of Mama and his brothers and the grove—and especially Sprite—he felt the little ache of missing them.

Bill interrupted Revver's thoughts. "Ya ready to get back to work, little guy?"

Revver jumped up, excited. ***"Vr-vr-vr-VRRROOOOM!"*** vibrated out of him.

Even after all this time, the sound sometimes caught Bill and the rest of the crew by surprise. Bill jumped, Trevor let out a little scream, and someone dropped a tool on the garage floor, making a loud **CLANK!** It was quiet for a second. Then they all looked up at Revver and laughed. The team loved Revver as much as he loved them.

They counted on Revver for lots of important jobs. He caught and collected lug nuts for Bill when Bill practiced tire changing. He helped Susan with wiring, and he helped Jeff with setup. He had learned the names of all the tools and fetched them when the crew needed something. And when he noticed something wrong or when he spotted danger (like the spring rubber or like the runaway tire that almost hit grumpy Jack near pit road), he alerted everyone with his thunderous *"Vr-vr-vr-VRRROOOOM!"*—the roaring engine sound that had earned Revver his name.

There were always new, exciting things for Revver to see and learn and do. And there were always LOTS of new things to learn NOT to do. New, important notes were always being added to Revver's brain burrow, the place where he filed all his important thoughts. Recently, he had to add **Exhaust pipes are NOT hiding places.** That mistake had shot Revver butt-first into the garage wall and knocked over a toolbox. The fur on his rear end was a little blackened for a while.

Bill had taught Revver to **Learn from Mistakes,** and Revver did his best. In fact, Revver was proud to say that he almost never made the same mistake twice. But somehow, Revver DID find all sorts of *new* mistakes to make.

Fortunately, the team loved having Revver around. They helped him clean up whatever messes he made, and they explained how to make sure it didn't happen again. They were very patient. UNFORTUNATELY, Jack was NOT patient. Jack liked to talk about his "smooth, spotless operation." So when things went wrong, Jack would yell. A LOT. His face would turn bright red, and the vein in his forehead would start throbbing.

"REVVERRR!!!" Jack would scream, and it always made Revver, and everyone else, jump.

Then Revver would look at Jack with big, sad eyes, and Jack would remember how Revver had saved his life—and how much he helped the team. Then Jack would stomp out the door, yelling, "Someone needs to clean up that mess RIGHT NOW!" And then he would poke his head back in and add, "And y'all need to keep the critter in line, or he's OUT!"

At night, Bill always fluffed up a pile of freshly washed shop towels in the garage and tucked Revver into bed. Then Bill would sit on the floor next to Revver and rub Revver behind the ears.

After a very mistake-y day, Bill would say, "Now, buddy, you made kind of a mess of things today. Let's try real hard to get through tomorrow clear and clean, okay? We don't wanna make a habit of pushin' ole Jack."

Revver wondered, *If Jack sends me "out," WHERE would I go?* Revver could not imagine. Leaving Bill and the race team was a horrible thought.

So when Bill asked Revver to try harder, Revver nodded, as best as a squirrel can nod. And that always made Bill laugh. "You sure are somethin', little guy!"

Once Bill turned off the lights and left the garage for the night, Revver would curl up and snuggle into the towels. He crossed his ankles together so he could feel the chain Sprite had given him. It made him feel safe.

Then Revver always dug deep into his brain burrow to remember one of his very first notes: Stop and think. And every night, Revver fell asleep promising himself that the next day, he would do just that. He'd stay out of trouble. He wouldn't get too excited or move too quickly or get too distracted. *Tomorrow*, he promised himself, he'd slow down and think things through.

But this was never easy. "Slow" was just not Revver's speed.

3

"Another race, another place," Bill said. And Revver knew it was time for them to pack up and leave, to head out for the next track and the next race. Bill carried Revver to the truck and gave him a few nice rubs behind the ears.

Most of the crew "flew" to the races. Revver tried to imagine them all, soaring through the

air like birds, and often wondered why he never saw them fly around the garage or at the track. He guessed it would be much faster. He would try to figure this out.

"Okay, little bud, I'll see you in a couple of days. You behave. Do *exactly* what Joe tells you to do and stay outta trouble. And I mean *exactly*. Okay?" As always, Revver nodded his best squirrel nod, and Bill gave him a gentle hug. Then Bill fluffed up a shop towel on the passenger seat and put Revver down gently with a few extra ear rubs.

Revver knew "rules." He knew the racing rules and his brain burrow rules. And he knew the rules of driving with Joe. Revver also knew what "exactly" meant. When they were working on a

car or doing wiring, things had to be just right. So Revver listened carefully to Joe and did *exactly* as he was told.

The car transporter, or the "hauler" as the team called it, carried the race cars to the next track. It was BIG and beautiful and rumbly. The tractor and the trailer together had TWENTY huge black tires. Revver had counted them. Everything was shiny and colorful, and the trailer had the team name on it, Jack Starr Motorsports, in big, bold letters. (Joe had read that to him.) The cars were the most important thing about racing, so Revver felt *very* important to be traveling with them.

Revver loved Joe. Joe was always so calm and kind.

While Joe drove the transporter, Revver often sat on his lap, looking out at the road ahead, along all the twists and turns and straightaways.

After they had driven awhile, Joe exited the highway and pulled into a gas station. "It's time

for a pit stop." Revver had learned on the first day of driving with Joe that it wasn't an ACTUAL pit stop, like during a race. This was a little disappointing at first. There was no jack lifting them up, no tire changing, no one wiping the front grill. This kind of pit stop meant that Joe was stopping the truck for fuel and to "git a cup o' joe." Revver got used to these kinds of more boring pit stops.

Joe told Revver, "Take yerself a poop break, little fella, and then get right back in the truck." Joe opened the passenger door, and Revver jumped out and ducked under the truck—for privacy. Then *plop-plop-poop!* He jumped onto the steps and right back onto his seat.

While Joe went inside, Revver looked out the truck windows, watching other trucks and drivers come and go. He always thought that his truck was more beautiful than any of the others.

After a while, Joe came back drinking a cup of something that looked like smoking motor oil. It didn't smell *quite* like motor oil, but it didn't smell *good*, either. *This must be a special kind of oil, to help humans run smoothly.* Revver had licked motor oil once, by mistake. It was awful. He did not care to try it again. He wasn't exactly sure why Joe liked the taste of this strange-smelling, smoking motor oil or why, when it was steaming in a cup, Joe called it "joe." Joe and *joe.* This was something else Revver would have to try to figure out.

Joe also brought back a bag with food for himself and some nuts and a bottle of water for Revver. Joe poured the water into a shallow cup and set the cup into a special holder between the seats. Then

Joe started the truck, picked up speed, shifted gears, and merged back onto the highway.

Joe and Revver sipped and snacked together as they rolled along.

"Ya wanna pull the horn?" Joe asked, smiling at Revver.

Revver nodded, as best as a squirrel can nod, and he jumped onto Joe's lap. It was a special treat when Joe let Revver pull the air horn. Revver did two light, happy little pulls: *Honk! Honk!* Joe said those were like saying, "Hello!"

The first time Revver tried pulling the air horn, the sound was so **BLASTING** that Revver shot up, jumped over Joe's shoulder, and hid behind the seats.

Joe had laughed until tears came out of his eyes!

But now Revver was an expert at the air horn, and it didn't scare him anymore.

Joe had explained that the long, loud pulls meant *danger*. It meant that Joe wanted someone to pay attention RIGHT NOW. Revver hoped he never needed to pull the air horn that way.

As Joe and Revver went along, Joe explained all sorts of things about the truck. At first, Revver learned simple things—like about the radio and air-conditioning and how Joe turned on the turn signals and the lights. This was all fascinating, because race cars didn't have any of those things! Then Joe taught Revver about shifting and the clutch and the gas pedal and the brake and the *Jake brake* (Revver loved the loud vibration of engine braking!) and the fifth wheel and all sorts of other things. Revver would nod again, to let Joe know that he loved to learn.

Revver knew that he was not allowed to touch *anything* on the dash. NOTHING. Joe told Revver that *exactly*. So Revver never touched anything. He was careful about that. He did not want to get into any trouble.

Revver did not like getting into trouble.

But sometimes, it just happened.

Revver loved looking out the windows of the transporter as the world went by. At night, there were
colorful lights along the road: white lights, red
lights, green lights. There were big, flashing signs
with many more lights. Sometimes, he would
see other trucks and cars with special lights on
them—spinning yellow lights or flashing red-and-
blue lights. It was all new and exciting.

The cars on this road were definitely *not* race
cars. They had no colorful decals. They did not
make delightful race-car sounds. They did not go
terribly fast. Revver wondered why any human
would choose a car that was NOT a race car. He
wondered if some humans did not *want* to drive

fast race cars, but the idea seemed so silly that he brushed it aside.

Now it was raining. Revver watched the wipers—*this way, that way, this way, that way*—clearing the rain from the windshield so that Joe could see his way. But from Revver's side window, everything looked blurry as the raindrops stuck to the glass. He tried to stick his head out to feel the wind, forgetting the window was there. *Ouch!* He banged his nose hard on the glass, and Joe shook his head and laughed.

Windows were irritating sometimes; Revver had never seen any in the grove. He was still getting used to them.

It started raining harder, and there was "traffic." At the track, traffic meant LOTS of cars going VERY fast, VERY close together. On the track, "traffic" was terribly exciting!

But this kind of traffic was NOT exciting. It was NOT fast. It was slow and boring. And soon, it was not just slow; it was STOPPED. *The only thing worse than **slow** is **stopped***, Revver thought.

There were some flashing red-and-blue lights up ahead. At first, they were interesting to watch, but Revver soon tired of them.

It was dark and gloomy. Joe let out a long, loud sigh. Revver and Joe listened to a song on the radio about a man who loved a Doris and a dog and a truck. The Doris did not sound nice. The Doris left and took the man's dog.

Revver pondered what a Doris was and how *anyone* could love a dog. Dogs did NOT like squirrels, so Revver did not like dogs.

But Revver *totally* understood loving a truck. *That human should stop worrying about the Doris and the dog and just drive the truck*, Revver thought. He was proud of himself for figuring out the man's problem.

Revver listened to the sound of the wipers *swish, swish, swish, swish*. He listened to the rain on the truck *patter-pat-pat-patter-patter-patter*. It started raining harder.

Joe sighed again, and the human kept on singing about his problems. And before he knew it,

Revver was curled up in the cozy passenger seat on his fluffy shop towel, fast asleep.

Later, when Revver woke up, the rain had stopped. The sky was brighter. The car transporter was parked. But Joe was nowhere in sight.

Revver was all alone.

Revver stood on his armrest. He looked out his window and then climbed onto the dash to look through the windshield.

This did not look like the kind of place where Joe usually made a pit stop. It was much bigger and a lot louder. Revver looked up at a huge, spinning sign with lights. There were lots of cars, coming and going. There were rows and rows of parked trucks.

Revver looked past the trucks and saw a building. It was MUCH bigger than the buildings Revver had seen before at rest stops and gas stations. When the door to the building opened, Revver heard music. He could hear humans, talking and laughing.

Where are we? he thought again. *Maybe we're at the track?* But Joe always woke him up when they got to the track, and Bill was always there to greet them. Nothing—and no one—here looked familiar.

Revver sat still and listened. He did not hear any racing sounds. He looked carefully at the other trucks. He did not see any other car haulers.

Joe ALWAYS gave Revver instructions: "Stay here—I'll be back in a sec" or "Sit tight, little guy—I'll see you in just a few." Now Revver had NO instructions and no idea where Joe had gone. How could he do *exactly* what Joe told him, if Joe had not told him *anything?*

Revver started to worry. *Is Joe okay? Why would he need to leave?* Revver was lonely—and scared. He waited for what seemed like a very, very long time. Finally, he made a decision. *I need to find Joe. Joe might need me!*

Revver's window was partly open. He jumped onto the armrest and squeezed out the window. Then he lunged for the side mirror, hanging off it before dropping onto the wheel well, sliding down to the truck steps, and hopping to the ground. He hid under the truck and took a look around.

He kept low, hurried toward the building, and watched.

Revver waited until a small group of humans went in, and then he trailed inside, close behind them. He quickly hid under some shelves while he looked around. *This is a big place!* It was busy and loud, and there were lots of things in this room that Revver had never seen before. He saw no sign of Joe.

Revver spotted a hallway. He crept along the wall, down the long hall. He turned a corner and found himself in a very bright room. Inside the room were many beige doors. *Maybe Joe is in HERE!* Revver peeked under one of the doors, hoping to find Joe. Instead, he found a human inside a very small room, sitting on a white chair.

"Aaaaaaaahhh!" When the human saw Revver, she shrieked so loudly that Revver, terrified, stumbled backward. He darted under another door to hide. He was panting. He took a deep breath to calm himself. There was no one inside *this* little room, but there was another white chair. *Wait a minute!* He recognized this chair, or *machine*, actually. Revver had seen it before! In fact, he had once started the engine on one of these machines and caused a big mess by hanging off the gas pedal! *It's called* . . . Revver thought hard, trying to remember. *A toilet! That's it!* He was very proud of himself for remembering the name. *Wait!* He quickly shuffled through his brain burrow and found an important note there: Toilets are not toys. Bill had taught him that!

Revver backed away from the machine, careful not to touch it. Bill would be proud of him! But Revver could not help thinking about the machine, because he liked to figure things out: he had never actually seen anyone ON a toilet before. *Oh!!!* With a flash, it was all starting to make sense! *NOW I understand! That middle part is . . . the driver's seat! But how does it move? Where are the wheels? And how do they steer it?*

These were things Revver would have to figure out later because now, he was starting to panic. *Where is Joe?!*

Revver scurried back down the hallway and peeked into another room. Humans sat at big, lighted machines where bells rang and buzzers buzzed and the humans hooted or shouted, "Yesss!" or "Oh, come on!" There were so many new sounds and SO many colorful, shiny, interesting things! It was dizzying! Revver went in and stayed low. He looked hard, because the room was sort of dark. Joe was not there.

Revver raced around the building. The more time that passed without finding Joe, the more nervous and frightened he felt.

He went into a giant area where people sat

eating at tables. *No sign of Joe.* He ran down hallways and into other rooms. *No luck.*

He ran into a room that felt steamy and where sounds echoed. He heard spraying water, and Revver felt his feet getting damp. He looked but only saw one very hairy, bubbly human standing under spraying water. It was not Joe.

Finally, he scurried back toward the entrance, which was even more crowded now. He hid and watched, trying hard to spot Joe, hoping *so hard* that he would see him.

Humans were picking things up and looking at them. Some put the things back and some took them up to another human behind a counter. He saw the human who had been on the driver's seat, on the *toilet*. She was not screaming now. He wondered why she was screaming before and decided that she must be a new driver. He remembered how scared *he* was when he had taken his first ride in the race car—so he understood.

Under the counter, Revver recognized something, all round and colorful and lined up on shelves. *Doughnuts!* he thought. Sometimes, someone on the crew would bring doughnuts to the garage, and one of them would always give Revver a small piece. He could smell the doughnuts under the counter, and Revver knew they were delicious. Suddenly, Revver was starving! He crawled low and carefully toward the doughnuts, waited until no one was looking, and quickly pounced to grab one. **OUCH!** *A window!* The doughnuts were behind a window! Revver hid and rubbed his head. This was the problem with windows.

Revver decided the doughnuts were on the *other* side of the window. He soon found his way around. He moved carefully. No one saw him! He crouched low and quickly grabbed a pink one with sprinkles. He ate the whole thing in just a few bites. Revver had never been given a WHOLE doughnut before! *Oh! It's sooo good!* He grabbed another one. Soon, that one was gone, too.

Revver was full. *Now I REALLY need to find Joe,* he thought.

But before he could follow that thought, something glinted in the middle of the room. Revver crept closer to inspect. Something tall was spinning. At first, it looked a little like a straight, white tree. Then, as a human walked away from it, the spinning slowed down, then stopped. Now Revver could see it was not a tree but a *tower* holding— *Hmm, what are THOSE called?* He tried to remember. *Sunglasses! That's it! That's what they're called!* Bill and the crew members wore them on their faces, outside, on bright days. Sometimes, when the sun was very strong, Revver wished he had some for himself! *This must be where they get them—they pick them off the tower! Humans pick sunglasses the way squirrels pick nuts!* This was new information. Humans were so full of mystery.

Revver moved in closer, and he looked up at the tower. He had never seen *so many* sunglasses! Some had chrome on them like engine parts, and

Revver could see himself in them. Some were colorful and sparkly. Some were dark and wide, like the kind the crew wore.

Revver sunk down low and pushed on the bottom of the tower. It slowly spun around again. As he looked up, all the colors whirled by. "Oh!" he whispered, mesmerized. He looked around to make sure no one had seen him, and he pushed it again. He played with the tower for a while, making it spin and watching the colors go around. It was so much fun that he forgot to be careful.

Higher up was a section of sunglasses that seemed much smaller than the rest. He gasped, "Those look like MY SIZE!" He could match the crew! They could all wear sunglasses together!

Revver looked carefully and noticed a sparkly blue pair. It was the *same* sparkly blue on the team's car! He LOVED that color! It always reminded him of a bright blue sky mixed with sparkling stars. *Perfect!* He tried reaching them, but they were too high. He stood on his tippy-toes. Still too high. He stepped onto the bottom of the spinner for a boost, but he was still not close enough to touch that beautiful pair of sparkly blue sunglasses.

Revver searched his brain burrow for help. *Stop and think.* So Revver stopped. And he thought. He studied the treelike tower. The places that held the sunglasses were like little branches up the trunk. *This will be easy!* After all, he'd climbed a tree MANY times. He planned his route and slowly started up the empty rungs—the spaces that did not hold any sunglasses—so that he had a gripping place for his paws.

At first, he moved slowly and carefully up the tower. His plan was working! But then the tower started to slowly rotate—trees never did that!

The sudden turning startled Revver, and he jerked—which only made the tower turn a little faster, which made Revver *climb* faster, which made the tower turn even faster. Soon, he was RUNNING up the tower, trying hard to stay focused on getting to the blue sunglasses. But now the tower was SPINNING really fast, and Revver was running sideways instead of up, just trying to stay on. He was starting to feel dizzy.

Sunglasses flew out of the tower, shooting like rockets in every direction. Revver could hear them hitting the floor—and other things around the room.

Revver lost sight of the blue sunglasses. He was just trying to keep a firm grip on the tower so he wouldn't fall off. Usually, he LOVED going fast, but this felt too twirly-whirly. He was so dizzy . . . He had never been dizzy before, and it was a new feeling. He didn't like it.

Now he could hear screaming as he whirled around. Was it the toilet driver? He wasn't sure.

Then the tower—and Revver—started *leaning* . . . *leaning* . . . *leaning* . . . until **BASH!** it tipped over! If Revver hadn't been buried in sunglasses, he would have seen the tower crash into a pyramid of motor oil containers, which smashed into a shelf of cola cans, which broke through the doughnut window. **CRASH!** went the window. Then *bang! Thud,*

thud, thud-thud-thud!—motor oil bottles and soda cans and shelves fell hard onto the ground. Some of them burst open with a *fizzzzz!* and circled around the floor, spraying soda everywhere.

Still SO dizzy, Revver unburied himself. He could feel his heart pounding in his ears. He sat still. He did not feel hurt, but he had trouble focusing his eyes on anything. The world was circling around and around, and he could barely see through all the mess. Then suddenly, across the room, Revver could focus just enough to see—*Joe!*

Joe looked very calm. His eyes met Revver's. Revver could not read the expression on Joe's face. Like always, Joe looked cool and relaxed.

Joe moved toward the door, carrying a big cup of steaming joe in his left hand. As Joe walked past Revver, he lowered his right arm, snatched Revver by the scruff, and quickly hid Revver under his jacket. Through the chaos, Joe was so swift and smooth that no one even noticed him—or Revver—leave.

Joe took Revver back to the truck. He set his cup down on the step of the truck and held Revver up, looking him right in the eyes.

"You okay there?" Joe looked concerned. Revver did not look good at all. "Are ya hurtin' any?"

Revver just stared back at Joe.

"Bud? You okay?"

Revver gave Joe a pitiful look and took a deep breath.

And then Revver threw up—bright pink—all over Joe's shoes.

The hauler passed car after car. Revver and Joe were back on their way to the next race. Revver still felt sick.

Joe shook his head. "Gracious, son, what got into ya back there?"

Revver just gazed at Joe with sad, watery eyes, barely lifting his head.

Joe snuck a peek at Revver, who looked pathetic. Joe was quiet for a minute, thinking.

"I mean, you know I always *come back*, right?"

Revver did NOT nod. Instead, Revver slowly shook his head—as best as a squirrel with a terrible tummy ache could answer.

Joe drove quietly for another while. "Did ya think I wasn't comin' back? Were ya *afraid?*" Revver thought. He remembered how he'd felt when he woke up in the truck, all alone. He had felt confused and lonely. He had been worried and very, very scared. He looked at Joe and nodded— the slightest, saddest nod.

Joe was quiet again. "Oh, bud," Joe said softly, shaking his head. Then he gave a long pause, thinking. "Okay, well, tell ya what. Here's the thing: I'm ALWAYS comin' back. I'm sorry I didn't wake you to tell you I was goin' in. That was my mistake. But you were sleepin' so sound, I figured I'd be back before you twitched a whisker. I left the window open for you to git some fresh air, and I didn't think a thing of it. But, little man, I'll tell ya—it's a big, big world out there, and you're a little guy. When I leave the truck, you need to stay here, where I know you're safe. Got it?"

Revver raised his head off the seat again and nodded another small nod. Joe reached over and rubbed Revver behind the ears, and then

Joe shook his head again and let out a very long sigh.

Revver rested in the passenger seat the remainder of the way. He was pretty sure he'd never eat a doughnut again.

Revver had never been sick before. Every rumble of the truck and bump in the road made his tummy ache more. When he tried closing his eyes, he felt like he was spinning again. It was a miserable trip.

As he rode along, he thought about Mama, his brothers, and Sprite. Feeling sick made him miss them terribly. He wished one of them could be with him now. He reached down and gently rubbed the chain on his ankle. It made him feel a little better. He was finally able to sleep.

By the time their truck approached the entrance to the track, Revver felt like his old self. Energy started to surge through him. Revver could almost SMELL racing. He could barely wait to see Bill and the crew!

Revver and Joe were in a long line of vehicles, all trying to get into the tunnel that led to the track infield. Revver stood up tall on his hind legs in the passenger seat to look out. Ahead of them were some car transporters and then a very long black car. It was the longest car Revver had ever seen!

In the side mirror, behind them, he saw the endless line of other haulers. He decided again that his team's truck, with its sparkly blue paint, was the best one.

Revver was getting impatient. *More traffic?* He began fidgeting around in his seat. *What's taking so long?* He did NOT like waiting. Now that he felt better, he just wanted to get *out* of the truck. He was ready for this trip to be over! But they were stopped. The only thing worse than *slow* was *stopped.*

"Settle down there, bud. Won't be too long." Joe was always calm and patient.

They waited longer. Revver was not happy.

They finally nudged forward a little bit. "Just that limo ahead of us now. It'll be our turn next."

Revver had never heard of "limo" before. He would remember this new word for the long black car.

He tried to be patient, but he was SO bored. This was taking *too long*. He felt like he had been sitting in the truck with Joe *forever*. He thought about the rainstorm and losing Joe and being afraid and feeling lost and growing dizzy and getting sick. He was *so glad* he felt better. He just wanted to forget about the whole thing and get back to work in the garage with the team! And he could not wait to see Bill!

Finally, it was the long black car's turn at the guard station. The car's driver was talking to the guard through his window. The driver handed over some papers. The guard looked at the papers and then went into the guard stand. He came out and talked to the driver again. This seemed to take a very, v-e-r-y long time. *What's taking so long?!*

Now Revver was almost hopping around the truck cab, unable to control his energy. He reminded himself of his brother Bounce, who could never sit still. Right now, Revver understood that feeling!

"Sit down, bud," Joe said. Joe sounded tired. It had been a long ride for him, too.

Revver tried to sit but found himself fidgeting again. *Once we get through the tunnel, we'll be in the infield! And then we'll be near the garage! And then we'll take out the cars. And then I'll see Bill!*

WHAT. IS. TAKING. SOOO. LONG?! Revver thought to himself while he BOUNCED.

Finally, the black car s-l-o-w-l-y inched forward, down the little hill, and into the tunnel. Revver could see its red brake lights, but the car was past the guard station. *Finally! It's our turn!*

Joe moved the truck forward. He stepped down out of the truck and walked up to the guard station and gave the guard some papers.

Revver was so excited, he could barely stand it! Instead of just fidgeting or hopping or bouncing, now Revver was JUMPING!

Joe was talking to the guard. Revver could still see the red brake lights of the long black car shining ahead of them, inside the tunnel. *Why is everything STALLED? Ugh.* Joe and the guard were still talking. Now Joe had his elbow on the truck, and he and the guard were laughing. Did Joe know this guard? Revver could not hear what they were saying, but he was getting very impatient. *Joe! Stop still talking! Stop laughing! Get in! We have to go!* Then Revver saw the guard give Joe . . . a cup of joe! This was too much! *What are they doing?!*

Revver leaped onto Joe's side of the car to try to get Joe's attention. He saw Joe take a long sip of the joe, and Revver couldn't stand it any longer. They needed to get going! Revver jumped onto the dash and pressed his face onto the windshield to look ahead. He jumped and jumped. He slapped his paws on the windshield; he was SO frustrated. He looked back to Joe, who just kept sipping and talking and laughing. This made Revver a little angry, and now he was REALLY jumping, all over the cab of the truck.

Ouch! Revver jumped so hard that he banged his head on the top of the cab! He fell forward and hit his face on the windshield. *Ugh! Windows!* Then he fell backward, and his foot caught on something on the front of the dashboard. He kicked his foot loose and slipped down again, catching something else. Whatever it was, Revver kicked that, too—hard. He was SO antsy and irritated. He jumped back up onto the top of the dash, still trying to get Joe's attention. Jumping, stomping, jumping.

Just then, Revver felt . . . something. He held per-fectly still. *Wait. Are we moving?* Very, very slightly, he thought he felt the truck move. He held his breath. It WAS rolling! The car transporter started to roll down the little hill—*WITHOUT JOE!*

Revver jumped back to Joe's side and banged on the window. Joe was still talking to the guard and laughing and drinking his joe. Now, Joe was standing right next to the guard station and was not looking at the car transporter, or Revver, at all.

Revver roared, *"Vr-vr-vr-**VRRROOOOM!**"*

For the first time EVER, no one heard him! The windows in the truck were shut. The sounds of all the engines from all the vehicles rumbled and echoed in the tunnel and drowned out Revver's yell.

The truck was JUST BARELY rolling forward, but it WAS moving. Revver was starting to panic!

Stop and think. Revver slowed himself down and tried to think. How could he get Joe's attention? Revver had an idea: he suddenly pounced and hung on the air horn. NOT two "hello" beeps but a long **HOOOOONK!**

Joe and the guard both looked up just in time to see the big rig rolling past the guard stand. It was starting to gain a tiny bit more speed down the small hill. Joe dropped his joe on the ground and started to run after the truck, but getting near a moving truck was too dangerous! Joe backed away. All he could do was watch.

Now Revver was really panicking! He must've kicked the brake release while he was jumping around! But what now?! What should he do?! *The brakes!* He jumped down to the brake pedal and stood on it, but he was too light. It wouldn't budge. He jumped back up to the windshield, looked down at the road ahead, and saw that the truck was coming closer and closer to the long black car—the limo—that sat at the bottom of the hill.

Whoever was in the back of the limo was now standing next to the car with their door open. They were looking ahead at the line, wondering, like Revver, what the holdup was about.

Revver pulled the air horn LONGER, and the person who was standing next to the black car got very startled. They turned and jumped away from the open car door and tripped and fell. Revver saw that it was a man. The man rolled and then landed on his bottom on the dirty pavement.

Revver looked down at the person on the ground. The person on the ground looked up at the truck. He met eyes with Revver. Then Revver recognized the person: it was . . . *JACK!*

CRR-UNCH!

It was not a high-speed crash. It was not *any-thing* like the crashes Revver had seen during races. But still, it was frighteningly LOUD. When the car transporter crashed into the limousine, the impact threw Revver off the windowsill and onto the seat. Revver quickly got back onto his feet and jumped up to see what had happened.

Even though the truck had not been rolling very fast, it WAS going fast enough to make a VERY BIG dent in the back of the limo. Its bumper and its trunk were all crunched up. Revver's heart sank. Revver could not see if there was also a dent in the truck, but he had seen enough crashes on the track to guess that the truck was probably banged up, too.

Revver knew: this was a BIG mistake.

On the ground a few feet away from the long black car, Jack was still sitting on the ground, screaming. Revver could not hear what Jack was saying, but he could see Jack's mouth moving and his angry red face and his throbbing forehead. The limo's driver came out of the car and walked right past Jack to check the back of the car. The driver put his hands on his face and shook his head.

Joe walked swiftly from the guard stand—the same way Revver saw him move to leave the truck stop. Joe helped Jack to his feet. Joe was calm and cool. Jack was not! Joe was nodding to Jack, and he put a hand on Jack's shoulder to try to settle Jack down. He gently nudged Jack back into the limo. Joe was still nodding. Jack was still screaming. Jack's arms were flying around, and his face was bright red. Joe shut the door of the limo with Jack inside. Jack rolled down his window so he could keep screaming at Joe.

Then Joe walked over to the limo driver, who was still looking at the rear bumper of his car and shaking his head. Joe talked to the driver and nudged him toward the driver's seat, patting the driver on the back as they walked. The driver shut the door, and the limo's brake lights went off.

Joe jumped onto the step and opened the truck door. Now Revver could hear bits and pieces of what Jack was screaming. ". . . blasted squirrel! . . . almost killed me! My transporter! . . . limo! He's OUT! . . . smooth, spotless operation . . . that squirrel! . . . I must've been CRAZY! He's OUT! OUT! OUT!" And then Joe sat down and shut the door, and Revver could no longer hear Jack yelling.

Joe said nothing. He just sat in the truck with his foot on the brake, waiting. Finally, the limo moved forward. It was making a scraping sound as it dragged its rear bumper behind it. Joe waited until the limo got farther ahead. Then Joe rolled the transporter forward, under the tunnel, up into the infield, and to the garage. Revver huddled low in the passenger seat, afraid that Joe would yell, too. Revver had heard a lot of screaming today. But, like always, Joe was calm and cool.

"Son," Joe said finally, as they parked, "I'd highly recommend you stay low and outta trouble for a while. Ole Jack will probably settle down, but I wouldn't guess it'd be too soon."

Revver looked at Joe and nodded, sadly. Revver did not like causing trouble. He didn't like disappointing Joe—or anyone.

Joe patted Revver's head. "Hey there, fella, it was an accident. Yer not the first youngin to get into trouble by havin' ants in yer pants. Don't be too hard on yourself. I'll explain everything to Bill. You know, we all love ya, Revver. You just gotta learn to be more patient."

Revver suddenly felt *sooo* tired, but he knew it was important to open his brain burrow and add, Be more patient.

Joe parked the truck and lowered the windows so Revver could have fresh air. Then Joe turned off the engine and jumped down to meet Bill, who was waiting to greet the truck—and Revver.

Revver pressed himself against the windshield to see.

Bill and Joe were talking very softly. Revver heard "brake release" and "front bumper" and knew that Joe was telling Bill what had happened with the limo. Then they were looking at the damage on the truck, and Revver saw Bill point his face to the sky with his eyes closed. He saw Bill let out a deep breath and run his hand over his hair. Revver knew Bill was not happy.

Then Joe and Bill spoke even more quietly. Revver could not hear anything more. But then he heard Bill shout, "Good *word*, Joe! What the heck happened to your *shoes*?!"

There was a big meeting in the garage—a "team meeting." Usually, Revver stood with the other crew members at team meetings. He was part of the team! But this time, he was not invited.

"You gotta hang out here this time, fella," Bill told him as he set Revver outside the garage and shut the door. Revver could tell that Bill did not want to look him in the eyes. Revver nodded as Bill walked away. Revver was sad and scared.

Revver waited outside the garage, unsure of what would happen. He knew this team meeting was about him. It was about the accident. It was probably about ALL of Revver's accidents.

Will I be "out"? If Jack gets rid of me, where will I go? What will I do? What will happen to me? he wondered, trying to imagine himself leaving the garage and going . . . *where?* He could not imagine. He remembered what Joe had said: *It's a big, big world out there, and you're a little guy.* Revver felt very small. His stomach felt twisty and sick— but he could not blame pink doughnuts this time. It was all his fault.

Revver crawled low and pushed one ear against the crack under the door to listen. He heard Jack yelling. Jack was doing a LOT of yelling! Jack yelled things like, ". . . enough is enough!" and ". . . at least ten grand worth of damage there!"

Then Revver heard Jack screaming at Joe for leaving Revver "unsupervised." Revver felt terrible that he got Joe in trouble.

Like always, Joe was calm and cool. "Jack, it was an accident. Accidents happen. You know that better than anyone."

Everyone started talking.

"He's such a help, Jack. He really is. He's just still learnin', that's all."

"We got the points lead because of him, don't forget."

"We've all messed up a time or two."

"He sure works hard, Jack."

"We sure love havin' him around."

"He's good for the team!"

"And it's not like you pay him or anything."

There was a small chuckle from the group.

All the nice things the team members were saying made Revver feel proud.

Revver heard Jack mumbling now. ". . . smooth, clean operation." And then Jack said, more loudly, ". . . and he almost killed me!"

"Jack, he pulled that horn to warn you."

"He wouldn't want nothin' to happen to ya."

"Yeah, Jack."

"You might not even be standing here at all if Revver hadn't gotten you outta the way of that tire a few weeks back."

"You can't forget *that*."

There was a very long pause. Then Revver heard Bill say, "Jack, he's family. You don't kick someone out of your family. That just ain't the way things are done."

I'm family, Revver thought. His heart felt full. He wished he could hug Bill.

There was another long pause. And then a grumble. It was Jack's grumble.

"Okay," Jack said, "y'all win. He can stay."

Revver didn't even realize he'd been holding his breath, but he let the air out with a big sigh of relief. A jolt of happiness zipped through him, ears to tail. "I can stay!" he whispered to himself.

Then Jack added, "But this is his **last chance**!"

There was quiet. And Jack raised his voice, almost to a scream. ***"And I mean it!"***

Revver heard footsteps coming toward the door, so he jumped out of the way and hid low. Jack stormed out of the garage, huffing.

12

Revver jumped into work with the crew and worked as hard—and as carefully—as he ever had. All week, he tried his very best not to make a single mistake. Whenever Jack came into the garage, Revver ducked down low and stayed out of sight. In a panic, he ALMOST jumped into the tailpipe, but he caught himself. He tried to be perfect. And there were no problems the entire week. *Not a single one!* Revver was proud of himself. He could tell the team was proud, too.

All that work made the week pass very quickly: Revver helped Susan with a new wiring project. He picked up lug nuts for Bill when it was time to practice tire changing. He fetched tools for the crew, and, when he wasn't busy helping, Revver tidied up around the garage, putting everything back in its place.

Finally, there was practice on Friday, qualifying on Saturday, and then the big race on Sunday. It was a great finish! Casey placed third and managed to avoid some messy crashes during the race. The team was still leading in points!

Jack spotted Revver near the pit wall during the race, and he gave Revver the faintest smile and nod. Jack was always in a good mood when things were going well on the track. Revver felt a little relieved, but his heart was still heavy. *One more mistake and I'm off the team. I have no more chances . . .* **Jack means it.**

Soon after the race ended, the team started packing up for the next track. *Another race, another place.* Revver found Joe standing near the car transporter, and he waited patiently until Joe was ready.

"Hey, now! There's my little travel buddy!" Joe was checking the cars in the trailer when he spotted Revver. "So, bud." Joe hesitated. He walked slowly toward Revver and kneeled down. "I guess you haven't heard"—Joe paused again—"there's been a change of plans."

Revver waited to hear more. He didn't understand.

Joe went on. "You won't be ridin' with me today." Joe bent over and scratched Revver behind the ears. "I'm sure gonna miss your company, fella."

Revver felt panic. Was he off the team?! Had he made a mistake?! He quickly thought through the last few days, trying to figure out what he might have done wrong to be *out*, but he could not think of *anything*.

"Oh, *there* you are!" Revver turned to see Bill walking up behind him, carrying a strange toolbox. Revver knew all the toolboxes, and this one was unusual; it only had one big door on it. He had never seen this one before.

Bill set the toolbox down on the ground in front of Revver and opened the door. Inside, the toolbox was completely empty—except for a fluffy shop towel on the bottom. "Okay, Rev, let's try this on for size." Bill nudged Revver into the box, the way Joe had nudged Jack into the back of the limo after the crash. Revver was not sure about the box, but he always trusted Bill, so he went inside.

The box was just a little bit bigger than Revver, and it was strange to be in it. It was dark. It smelled odd. Revver decided he did not like being in the box, and he turned around to get out.

But just then Bill shut the door! He lowered a latch and turned it. Revver was locked inside!

The front door of the box had a wire window, and Revver pressed his face against it to look out. He stood perfectly still on the towel and waited to see what would happen next, heart pounding.

Bill lifted the box and held it up to his face. Revver could see Bill through the wire window. "I know it's not too great in there, bud," Bill said with a kind voice, "but it's the rules."

The rules? What rules?! Revver's mind went through all the racing rules he knew—whether their car could pit on a yellow flag, how many people were allowed on a pit crew . . . he knew what all the flags meant, and why drivers or teams got penalties, and when they could use their backup car, and what happened during inspection. None of those rules seemed to explain why Revver *was locked in a box*!

Revver dug through all his brain burrow notes, top to bottom, trying to see if he had broken any of *those* rules. He had not sprayed himself with brake cleaner or played with a toilet or tripped the fuel man. He had learned from his mistakes! He was trying to be more patient . . . !

Revver shook his head frantically to tell Bill that he did not understand.

Bill tried to explain. "Jack thinks that I'm the best one to look after you and keep you outta trouble." Revver was still confused. He shook his head again. "So you're gonna be in the crate awhile today."

Is this a punishment? Revver kept shaking his head. He started pleading with Bill out loud. *"But*

why? Why do I have to stay in here? What did I do?!"
Revver kept asking, hoping that, just this once,
Bill could understand Squirrel as well as Revver
understood Human.

"Dude," Bill said and chuckled a little, "you
remember that I don't understand a word you're
sayin', right?" Bill did *not* understand Squirrel, but
he knew Revver well enough to see that he was
confused and *very* unhappy. It broke Bill's heart a
little. Bill whispered, "Don't worry, little fella. Yer
not in trouble or anything."

Revver sat down on the fluffy shop towel, anxious, waiting for more information.

"You're gonna be *flyin'* to the next race—with
the team."

13

I'm flying with the team! I'll be with the team! And Bill! Revver was excited! But then he was nervous. He did not know how to fly! Did Bill know this? Would Bill be disappointed that Revver did not know how?

And this . . . *crate*?! Revver tried to imagine flying through the sky with the team, but he could not imagine doing it in the box. Maybe Bill would carry the box as he flew through the sky? But how would Bill flap his wings—or his arms—if he was holding the box? It was all very confusing.

Revver did not have much time to imagine. Very quickly, the whole crew got into several cars. Revver, in the crate, was on Bill's lap. Bill turned the front of the crate toward the window so Revver could look out, but the wire window made it hard to see. He suddenly missed riding in the car transporter with Joe, where he was free to move around. Revver did not care about *the rules*. He did not like being in this box!

And then Revver heard someone say, "The airport." Then he heard someone else say, "Delta." Hmm . . . Revver had not heard of these things before. He listened for more information.

After a while, the car stopped, and Bill and the others got out. Revver could only see little bits through the crate, but he heard a LOT of new sounds. He heard VERY loud engines. He heard horns honking. He heard cars stopping and starting, and he heard . . . *What was that?* Some kind of loud whistle. He heard a lot of yelling. He heard human feet, running.

Bill carried Revver's crate and walked with the others. Revver felt like they were moving very quickly. Now they were inside. It was much cooler in here, and there were a lot of lights—and new sounds. Revver heard more feet walking and running. He heard a loudspeaker, but the announcer was not talking about racing. He heard the announcer say something about "security" and "it is against regulations for anyone to . . ." But the sounds of people talking and rolling wheels and shoes tapping on the shiny floors were distracting. Revver could see many, many, many feet. Was this the *airport?* It was the biggest inside place Revver had ever seen, and it was so loud and busy! It felt terribly exciting.

Then Bill and the others stopped walking. They were standing in a line. Bill knelt down next to the crate and opened the door. "Buddy, I know this is gonna feel a little strange, but you need to wear this for a short bit. You need to stay right with me and not cause a fuss. You need to walk with me through security." *Security. There's that word again,* Revver thought.

Bill put a cord around Revver's neck and led Revver out of the crate. It was a strange feeling to have this around his neck. Bill was holding the end of the cord and leading Revver in the line. It did not feel good, but Revver stayed close to Bill so he would not feel it pulling on his neck.

Bill put the crate onto a moving track that sucked it into a machine. Then Bill picked up Revver and walked through a metal doorway.

"Whoa, whoa, whoa," a human in a uniform said. "That's a squirrel."

"Yes, ma'am," Bill said *very* politely. "Is there a problem, ma'am?" Bill asked.

"IS THERE A PROBLEM?" The human was talking very loudly. "YOU CAN'T BRING WILDLIFE INTO THE AIRPORT, SIR! Ed!" the human yelled out. "Ed, get over here and help me with this." Another person came over. Ed was wearing the same uniform as the first human. Ed was scratching his head.

*Am I **wildlife?*** Revver wondered. He did not *feel* very wild, **especially** at the moment.

People in the line behind Bill and Revver were starting to huff and complain.

"What's the holdup?!"

"My flight boards in twenty minutes!"

"Come ON!" someone else shouted. "Just let 'em go through. He has a crate."

Ma'am and Ed made Bill and Revver stand off to the side so the complaining humans could pass by. More people in uniforms surrounded them. One human came over with a big book of papers and started looking through it. Another stood next to them, typing quickly on a computer.

Some members of the team passed by. "You gonna be okay there, Bill?" Trevor asked.

"Oh, sure. We're fine."

"Gate D41," Susan told Bill.

"Okay, see you there. Hopefully we won't be long."

But Revver was scared. *What's happening?* he thought.

"Don't worry, little fella. It's all gonna be okay," Bill said, as if he could read Revver's mind. "We just have to stand here and be patient." Revver remembered his newest note, **Be More Patient.** Revver studied Bill's face, but Bill did not look patient. He looked worried.

14

Someone in a different, fancier uniform walked up to Bill and Revver. "So we have a problem here," the human said. "You KNOW that's a squirrel, right?"

Before Bill could say anything, Revver nodded—as best as a squirrel can nod. The human jumped back. "Whoa. Did that squirrel just NOD at me?"

"He's, um, a pretty special squirrel, sir. He's, um, *trained*," Bill said finally.

Revver pressed his cheek against Bill's to say "thank you." Revver was not sure he was *trained*, but he loved that Bill thought he was special. *Tell him I'm family!* Revver thought.

The man stared at Revver. He looked doubtful. "Is that true, fella? Are you *trained*?"

Revver lifted his head and nodded again. Now all the humans in uniforms were looking at him. Some had their mouths hanging open.

The one who Bill had called "sir" was quiet and just looked very closely at Revver. "Will ya shake my hand?"

Revver thought this was a strange request, but he'd seen humans shaking hands before. So Revver held out his paw to the man, and the man took two fingers and shook Revver's paw.

Oohs and *ahhs* traveled through the group.

"Check this out, y'all!" Sir said loudly. Then he asked, "How 'bout a high five?" and held up a hand in front of Revver's face. Revver had seen high fives many times with the crew. He tapped the hand with his paw. Some of the humans in uniforms clapped, and some laughed and cheered. Revver found this odd. *These humans are easy to please.* They never even saw him help with wiring or spark plugs.

"What a cute little thing he is!" said the one Bill called "ma'am." "I just wanna take him home with me!"

Revver was startled. He sat up tall. *I can't go home with you! I'm on the team!* Revver began shaking his head very quickly to tell the human that he could NOT go home with her.

Everyone laughed. "Oh, don't worry, fella. I'm just kiddin' around. It looks like you're pretty attached to this guy here," Ma'am said, pointing to Bill.

Revver nodded and moved closer toward Bill. A few humans chuckled and one said, "*Aww*, look at that."

Finally, the human with the computer said, "Well, I can't believe it, but I don't see anything in here sayin' 'no squirrels.' What about you, Bob?"

The human with the big book of papers shook his head. "Nothin' here, either."

Ma'am shrugged and said, "Ya learn somethin' new every day, I guess."

"Well, it seems like you and your trained squirrel are good to go," said the human in the fanciest uniform. "We won't keep you any longer. Y'all have a good flight." He was holding Bill's toolbox and held it open toward Revver. Bill removed Revver's cord and set Revver gently into the crate and onto the shop towel. Bill gave Revver a little ear rub and then shut the door.

"Thank you, sir," Bill said politely.

"Where you headed?"

"Charlotte," Bill said.

"Gate D41," Sir said.

Charlotte! That's where we're going! We're flying to Charlotte! Revver knew he would remember that word; it just sounded so exciting!

"Have you traveled with him before?" asked the human, handing Bill the crate.

"Nope, this is the first time." Now Bill was holding the crate.

"Well, I'm guessing this'll be quite the adventure for 'im, then. You two have a good trip."

"Thank you," Bill said again.

An adventure! Revver thought. *How exciting!*

15

"All right, Revver, let's just double-check that gate number," Bill said, standing in front of a huge electric board with words. "Yep, D41. Way over to D. That's gonna be a long haul."

Bill bent over so Revver could see him through the window of the crate. "You ready?" Revver nodded. Bill smiled for the first time since they went into *security*.

Bill and Revver walked and walked. They stopped and waited for a shuttle train. While they waited, the announcer kept saying, "Shuttle train to D gates arriving. Please stand clear of the doors," over and over. *This IS exciting!* Revver thought.

The doors opened, and Revver and Bill got in. Bill sat down and held Revver's crate with the door facing the shuttle window, making sure that Revver could look out. But when the shuttle started to move, it jerked—hard. Revver was tossed from the front of his crate to the back. "Oops, sorry, fella. I shoulda warned you about that." Bill chuckled.

Revver righted himself. The shuttle was *very* fast, and Revver loved it! But it was frustrating that the crate window was so small. Revver could see only the tiniest bit through the wires in the front.

The shuttle stopped, and Bill and Revver got out. Bill walked a very long time. They took some electric stairs up . . . and then down. Then they stood still on an electric floor that moved them forward. Then they walked more. Finally, Bill said, "Here we are. See that up there, Revver? D41. That's our gate."

This did not look like any kind of "gate" that Revver had ever seen. It was just an open room, filled with chairs and people. Bill walked into the room and over to a huge window. He turned Revver's crate around so that he could see. Outside, giant white machines rolled around. Bill knelt down next to the crate and whispered, "See those, bud? Those are airplanes! When they tell us it's time, we'll get inside one of those. Then we'll go UP into the sky, and when we land, we'll be in Charlotte. See that? Look at those; aren't they awesome? Now watch back there"—Bill pointed in the distance—"that one's about to take off. Watch!"

Revver's mouth had been hanging open in disbelief from the second Bill started talking. *Airplanes! THAT'S how they do it! So THAT'S how we're going to fly! We're going into an airplane!* Revver had seen airplanes fly over the track before races, all together, like birds in formation. He never realized that there were HUMANS inside! Revver watched the engines of the plane start up and take the white metal bird *up-up-up!* into the clouds. Now Revver felt a little silly, imagining Bill and the crew flying through the sky, flapping their arms.

He and Bill watched two more planes wait in line and then take off into the sky.

"It's amazing! They're like race cars for the sky! Wait until I can tell Sprite about this!" Revver whispered to himself. He thought back to his sister for a moment. He tapped the braided cord around his ankle and felt an ache that he could not share this moment with her. Then he imagined Joe driving the car transporter to Charlotte, and he felt badly for Joe. *Poor Joe.* He did not get to fly through the sky with the team in one of those big white birds. Revver wondered if Joe knew about airports and airplanes.

After a while, Bill found a seat near some of the other crew members. It was very loud and busy in the gate room. On loudspeakers, humans were calling out numbers. And they said things like "last call" or "boarding now." Revver was getting antsy. He felt like he'd been in this crate a very long time. He started to fidget.

"Hold on there, bud," Bill said in a soft voice. "We have to wait. Pretty soon they'll call us to board the plane, and you'll get to feel how fast it goes when it takes off! It feels like a ride in a race car! Won't that be fun?"

Revver nodded, a very enthusiastic nod, which made Bill laugh again.

"Just hang on, fella. It shouldn't be long."

But it WAS long. They waited and waited. Revver did NOT like waiting. He tried to curl up with his shop towel and go to sleep, but he was too excited about riding in the plane. He stretched and looked out the little window of his crate and fidgeted and twitched and turned and then did it all again and again. Revver heard Bill sigh as he stretched out his legs. *Bill is tired of waiting, too.*

Suddenly, all the lights around them turned off! Revver heard some humans gasp, and then everything got quiet. It was dark, except for some dim light coming through the windows. Then some smaller lights went on.

Revver listened closely. Now he could hear thunder. Then he noticed the sound of raindrops against the nearby windows. It was raining—hard.

After a few seconds, the big lights came back on and all the sounds—the people talking and the loudspeakers calling out numbers and the sounds of feet walking and wheels rolling on the floors—started up again.

Then Revver heard a loudspeaker that sounded closer than the others. "Attention, passengers for flight 2577 to Charlotte, scheduled to depart at three fifteen. We're sorry to inform you that, due to severe storms, our incoming plane has been delayed. Air traffic control has grounded all flights. We will keep you updated as soon as information is available."

People all around Revver sighed and groaned. Even Revver groaned—a sort of squirrely chirpy kind of groan. Revver heard Susan ask Bill, "Hey, you wanna go with us and grab a bite?"

Bill sighed. "Sure, why not. Looks like we're stuck here awhile."

Stuck here? Stuck HERE?! IN THE CRATE?! Revver had seen the rain make slow traffic for Joe. He had seen rain cause delays at the track. He hated that the racing had to stop when it rained. He hated waiting for the rain to go away. Now he was stuck in a crate at the airport—because of rain.

"I hate rain!" Revver shouted. No one paid attention. And none of the humans spoke Squirrel anyway.

Revver thought about Joe. Even when it was raining, Revver could still move around in the cab of the hauler with Joe. Revver decided that Joe probably knew enough about airports to want to drive in the truck. Revver was starting to not care about flying in an airplane. He wished he were back in the truck with Joe.

It was going to be a very long, very boring day.

16

Bill and the team walked around the airport and found a place to eat. Bill put Revver under the table. It was dark and boring, but Bill put some peanuts, fruit, and water into the crate. Revver nibbled on a peanut, but he wasn't feeling hungry. He just felt glum.

"Hello, squirrel!"

Revver jumped at the high-pitched squeak.

Right in front of the small crate window sat a mouse munching on a large crumb in its front paws.

"Oh!" Revver pepped up. "Hi, Mouse!" Revver felt a little happier to meet someone new.

"Lucky!" The mouse looked at Revver.

Revver looked down at his pile of peanuts. He guessed Mouse wanted some, too. "Oh! Would you like some peanuts?"

"No. I mean, my NAME is *Lucky*."

"Oh. I thought you meant that I was *lucky*—because I have peanuts."

"Well, of course, I do LOVE peanuts, but I can get them when I want them. Someone is always dropping peanuts in the airport."

"Wait. You LIVE here? At the airport?"

"Yes! That's why I'm *Lucky*! I love living here! It's SUCH an exciting place—so many delicious things to eat, so many warm, cozy places to hide . . . I just can't imagine a more wonderful place! Don't you think so?"

Revver sighed. "Maybe. It's just not very *wonderful* if you are locked in a *crate*."

"Hmm." The mouse was thinking. "Before I came here, I saw squirrels all the time—outside, in trees. I've seen other animals here in those." Lucky pointed to the container holding Revver. "But, well, now that you mention it, I've never

actually seen a *squir-
rel* in a box. I mean, a
crate."

"Well, I've never
actually seen a mouse in
an airport."

"Fair enough."

"How did you get here?
Were you in a crate, too?"

"Not exactly. One moment, I had climbed into
a container to munch on some *delicious* strawber-
ries. I must have fallen asleep because, when I
woke up, the container was closed. I nibbled my
way out, and here I was!"

"I wish I could nibble my way out."

"Where are you going in that box?"

"Crate."

"I mean, *crate.*"

"In an airplane. To get to Charlotte. But it's taking an awfully long time."

"Ah." Lucky stopped eating and looked thoughtful. He sniffed the air. "Rain?" he guessed finally.

"Yes."

"I don't like rain."

"Neither do I."

"That's another reason I love the airport: no rain in here!" Lucky declared. "There is nothing more pathetic than a wet mouse."

Revver jumped. "*Please* tell me more about the airport! I'm missing *so much* being in *this*." Revver pointed to either side of his crate with his paws.

"Oh, it's magical! SO many things to see and smell—and eat! The eating is the BEST! A mouse is never hungry at the airport! And you know, I've been here a very long time, but I STILL haven't even seen all of it! There is something new around every corner!"

"It sounds so . . . *exciting!*" Revver said.

"Oh, IT IS! And everything at the airport moves so wonderfully *fast!* It's never boring!" Lucky looked at Revver's sad face. "I'm sorry that you are stuck in there."

Revver sighed again. "Me too." Ever since he was a baby squirrel, he loved fast, exciting things. That was why he *loved* racing and cars so much. That was also why he *hated* sitting in a crate so much.

"But you know." Lucky perked up. "It's probably best that you are safe in there, in that box—I mean, *crate*. The airport is wonderful"—Lucky lowered his voice—"but it can also be quite *dangerous* when you're new at it."

Revver's ears perked up. Something about the way Lucky said *dangerous* felt thrilling! "Like what?! WHAT is *dangerous* at the airport?"

"Well, the humans, of course. Fast, stomping feet are *everywhere*! And all those boxes on wheels! And small humans running! And big humans pushing small humans in carts! SO many dangers! It took me a while to learn how to move around without getting stepped on." Lucky looked at Revver. Revver stared back, waiting for more.

"Best to stay near the walls," Lucky said finally, sounding very wise.

"Oh!" Revver said, as if this were important news. "What else?" Revver asked, breathy and wide-eyed.

"Well, then there are . . ." Lucky moved in closer, his nose pressed up against the crate window. It was very dramatic.

"Yes? *What?*"

Lucky whispered, "The Stick Shakers."

Revver gasped. "The Stick Shakers!" He had no idea what that was, but it sounded dangerous—*and thrilling!*

"Yes. The Stick Shakers. They are always out to get us!"

"They ARE?!" Revver held his front paws over his mouth.

"Well, I'm not sure about YOU. But definitely ME. All mice, actually. The Stick Shakers HATE mice."

"But . . . *why?*" Revver could not imagine. Mice in the grove were always so small and harmless.

"I'm a *rodent*."

"What's a *rodent?*"

"I have no idea."

Revver thought about this. He felt like he had heard that word before, but he wasn't sure.

"And sometimes, *birds* fly into the airport. I've seen the Stick Shakers try to get them, too."

"Really?!"

"Yes."

"And . . . *then* what happens?"

"Well, of course, they never can. The birds fly away, naturally. And anyway, birds are just too smart for the Stick Shakers."

"If they are smart, WHY do birds come into the airport in the first place?"

"Well, of course, all the food here . . . *and* . . ."

"And *what?*"

"To observe."

"Why?"

"To gather *information*."

"Why?"

"To learn."

"To learn . . . *what?*"

"Well, everything."

"*Everything?!*"

"Yes."

17

Soon, Bill and the others scooted their chairs away from the table. Lucky hid, low and tight against the wall. He was barely visible. "Well, it looks like you're going. Good luck with the rain delay. Hopefully you won't be stuck in there too long."

"It was nice to meet you . . . ," Revver said. But his voice trailed off as Lucky scurried away. Revver watched him go. He was SO envious of Lucky being able to run free to explore in this big, interesting, *fast* place.

Bill carried Revver and the crate around the airport some more. Bill opened the crate door and put Revver's leash on him. *It feels so good to be walking!* Bill led Revver to a place outdoors so Revver could poop—*plop!-plop!-poop!* But then Revver had to go right back into the crate.

They went back to gate D41. They sat and sat and waited and waited. Then the loudspeaker told them, "Attention, passengers to Charlotte. Your gate has been changed to E14."

Everyone groaned and got up and walked and took a shuttle and more electric stairs and more moving floors and walked again and then stopped at E14. As best as Revver could tell, E14 looked almost exactly like D41. He did not understand the point of this.

Bill set down Revver's crate on the floor at E14. Revver was impatient and bored and antsy and fidgety. He looked out his small window. He thought about Lucky, running around, free to explore. He thought about all the peanuts and other snacks Lucky was enjoying. Now Revver was grumpy.

Then some people sat down next to Bill, and Revver spotted another box—a crate—that looked A LOT like his own!

Revver looked into the box next to him. It was a kind of animal Revver had never seen. It was white and SO puffy, and it was licking one of its paws. It reminded Revver of a fluffy cloud. He watched the creature very closely. *What IS it?*

The creature looked up and noticed Revver watching. "Excuuuuse me?" he said in a long, low voice. The creature sounded annoyed. "Haven't you ever seen a *cat* before?"

"Cat." Revver said it out loud so he'd remember what it was called. The cat huffed and rolled his eyes. He went back to licking himself.

Revver had seen a mountain lion once, from far away, when he lived in the grove. But the mountain lion was MUCH, MUCH bigger than this animal, and it was not white and poofy. But there was *something* about this "cat" that reminded Revver A LOT of that mountain lion, even though this creature in the crate was barely bigger than Revver. *Maybe it's a baby!*

"Are you a baby?" Revver asked.

"You're insssulting!" the cat hissed and glared at Revver.

Revver did not know what "insulting" was, but the hissing made Revver jump back.

"Um, no I'm not. I'm a squirrel."

"I know what you are, *rodent*. I just can't BELIEVE that anyone would want to OWN you." The cat started licking his other paw.

Revver did not know how to reply. *Someone owns me?* And he still did not know what "rodent" meant, but the cat had said it in a way that *did not* sound nice.

Revver waited a moment and then decided to explain. "I only thought you might be a *baby* because you remind me of a mountain lion. Except you are smaller."

The cat stopped licking himself and looked up at Revver with wide green eyes. Revver backed away.

The cat jumped to attention and pressed against his crate window, closer to Revver. "A ***mountain lion*****?!**" The cat seemed excited. It scared Revver.

Revver was afraid to answer. "Y-y-y-yes?"

The cat suddenly seemed very happy. "Of course! *Of course* I remind you of a *lion*! The KING of the jungle! The BIGGEST of the big cats!"

I said **MOUNTAIN** lion, Revver thought—but something told him not to interrupt the cat.

"I'm so fierce and handsome and . . . *majestic*! You are so, SO right! You would NEVER call me *an average house cat*, would you?" The cat puffed himself up, trying to appear larger.

"N-n-n-no?" He was not sure if he got the right answer. The cat talked very quickly and used a lot of words Revver had never heard before.

"Thank you, *squirrel*! Of course, you're right. I am NOT average. I'm INCREDIBLE! I've won lots of awards, *you know*."

"Oh!" **Now** Revver was impressed. "Have you won *racing trophies*?"

"Race . . . NO! Of course not! Cats don't *race*, you *animal*! I've won awards for my . . . *purr-fection*!" The cat gestured to himself as if this was an obvious fact. Then he pointed up toward the top of the crate with one paw. "I belong to THEM. Of course, they adore me. Because, as you said, I'm *spectacular.*" The cat went back to licking himself.

Revver was pretty sure he had not called the cat *spectacular,* because he did not know what *spectacular* meant. He changed the subject. "Um, excuse me, um, *cat* . . ."

"You may call me *Lou,*" said the cat, as if he were giving Revver a present.

"Um, okay then, um, *Lou.*" Revver tried to remember what he wanted to ask. "Aren't you bored in your crate? I've been in here for SUCH a long time. I'm starting to get grumpy. I'm having trouble sitting still. How *do* you stay so calm and happy in there?"

Lou continued licking his paws. He did not look up.

"That's *because,* rodent . . . Oh, I'm sorry, how rude of me. Do *you* have a name?"

"They call me Revver, because I can make a very loud sound, like a car . . ."

"I don't care."

"Oh."

"Anyway, *Revver*," Lou hissed the name like an insult, "I'm NOT bored because I'm *domesticated*. And you, of course, are *not*."

Domesticated. Revver had not heard this word before.

"I don't know what that means."

Lou rolled his eyes and shook his head. He was very annoyed. "It means that I always manage to find some way to amuse myself because I have

interesting *ideas* to keep my brain busy. Basically, I'm just much smarter than you."

Then Lou's eyes flashed as if he had a wonderful thought! He stopped licking and looked right at Revver. "And, you poor, *poooor* thing, it means that YOU should NOT be kept in a crate. It's just not good for you. You should be free to run around a bit."

"I should?"

"Of course you should. You said it yourself."

"I did?"

"Certainly."

"But what about *the rules?*"

"What rules?"

"The a*irport* rules."

"Oh, *those.* I'm not telling you to *break* any rules. I'm just suggesting that you *bend* them a little. Get out, run around. The airport is a wonderful, exciting place! So much to see! It will be good for you! Then return to your crate after you've gotten some exercise. You'll be *so much* happier, and your human will never even know you are gone." Lou pointed up toward Bill. Revver could hear Bill snoring lightly in the chair above him. "He will just be *so very happy* at how CALM you will be on the plane, because you've let off a little steam."

Revver DID always want to make Bill happy. And the idea of getting out of the crate for just a short run made Revver so excited . . .

"I don't *know* . . ." Revver hesitated.

"Fine. It's up to you. But we could be here all night. So, if you want to stay in that crate *all night* . . ."

"All night?!"

"I have been in airports many, many times, my friend," said Lou. "And once, I was in an airport with *them*"—Lou pointed up to the top of the crate again—*"an entire night!"*

Revver could NOT imagine being in this crate all night! He panicked at the thought! The **Be More Patient** note floated down from Revver's brain burrow. He saw a glimpse of it pass before him, but it only made him irritated to think about it. He punched it away angrily.

"Well, I *would* like to run and explore a little. This seems like such a fast, *exciting* place! But . . ." Revver sighed. "I'm locked in, anyway." Revver pushed on his door to show Lou that it would not open.

"Well, you are very lucky to have found me today, then," said Lou. "Here, *rodent*—I mean, *Revver* . . ." And with that, Lou pushed a front paw through the wires in his own crate and unlocked Revver's.

"But . . . you could unlock *your own* crate!" Revver said. He was very impressed with Lou.

"Of course. But why would I? I'm perfectly happy in here."

"Because you're . . ."

"Domesticated," said Lou.

"And I'm . . . ?" Revver said.

"Certainly *not*."

18

Revver poked his nose out of his crate. He looked through the chairs and legs and feet and started to plan a path through for a little run. He was feeling happy and excited for the first time in *hours*.

"But wait!"

"What?" He turned to Lou.

"You need to pay me, *of course*. When someone provides a service to you—as I did when I unlocked your crate—a payment is required." Lou pressed himself against the window of his crate and stared at Revver with wide green eyes. "Of course, everyone who's *domesticated* knows this."

Revver knew a little bit about *payment*. Sometimes, through the window of the truck, Revver had seen Joe pay for gas and snacks in the store.

Revver looked down, nervous.

"I—I—I . . . I don't have anything to pay you."

"Of course you do. That nice orange trinket on your ankle will do just fine."

"This is from my . . . I mean, this is *special*."

"Oh, it's *special*! Even better."

"I can't give this to you."

"Have it your way. Get back into your crate."

"But . . ." Now that Revver was out, he certainly did not want to go right back in. "But what if I *don't*?"

"Then I will scream the loudest, most horrible screech imaginable. It will wake your human immediately, I promise you that. And then you will go *nowhere*—and I don't think your human would be too pleased to see you out of your crate."

Revver looked at Lou, stunned.

"And anyway, I only want to *borrow* it. You know, until you return."

Revver's mind swirled.

Lou set himself on his back paws, the way Revver planted himself when he revved his loudest. Lou took a deep breath and opened his mouth wide.

"Okay! Okay!" He did not take time to think. Revver quickly pulled the braided orange chain from around his ankle—the one that Sprite had woven so beautifully just for him, the one he had not taken off since Sprite gave it to him. He took off the chain, and he gave it to Lou.

"Here," Revver said, hastily pushing it through Lou's crate. "But I'll be right back."

"*Of course* you will. I mean, how far could you possible go *in an airport?*"

Revver started to make a dash out of gate E14 and toward the center hallway where the lights were brighter.

He thought he heard Lou laughing as he left. It was not a nice laugh. But Revver did not stop to think about it.

19

Revver sped off as fast as he could run. *Front paws, back paws, front paws, back paws.* He wove his way through walking feet and rolling boxes, being careful to stay near the walls so no one would see him. But everyone was in such a hurry, no one even noticed him.

This is so much more exciting outside that crate! He found bits of dropped food—a few pieces of pop-corn, a french fry, and a trail of Cheerios left by a little human. He found a rubbery blob under a chair that smelled fruity and good, but he could not unstick it from the chair. He licked it—but it didn't taste like much. He decided to leave it.

He smelled all sorts of things. His nostrils filled with the yummy things that Bill and the crew had let him sample in small tastes: pizza and tacos and hamburgers. Revver's little mouth watered. He passed a store that smelled entirely like the piece of candy bar that Susan had broken off for him. He passed a little stand that roasted nuts. (Luckily, a delicious few were dropped nearby!) He walked by other stands that sold shiny things that caught his eye: gleaming buttons and chains. He walked by a colorful store that smelled like doughnuts—his insides churned unhappily, remembering the pink doughnut disaster. He went by without even peeking in.

He saw lots of people standing in line, and he knew by the smell that they were waiting for "joe"—the steaming motor oil that Joe drank in the truck. *Ugh. I will NEVER understand how they* **like** *that stuff!*

He saw a place that sold nothing but—*sunglasses!* Revver peeked in, hiding low against the walls, in the corner. He had never seen SO MANY sunglasses before! There were sunglasses on the walls, lined up almost to the ceiling. There was a human behind a counter. The counter was filled with sunglasses. And there were THREE spinning towers of even MORE sunglasses. Revver remembered the spinning tower accident from the truck stop. He decided that he would NOT try climbing any of the towers. But still, he looked hard to see if there was a small, sparkly blue pair, like the ones he had seen at the truck stop. He looked for a long time, but he did not find any. He moved on.

He passed a little store that smelled sweet— and felt chilly. He ventured in, but he could not see anything except a high counter and a human scooping out *something*. He hid under a small round table with swirly metal legs. Nearby, someone spilled a big drop of something white, with black specks. When the coast was clear, Revver ventured over to sample it: it was cold and creamy. It was probably the most delicious thing Revver had ever tasted! He waited. There were other drops from other humans at other tables: one was green with black specks. One was orange. One was white with colorful pieces. *Each one is so good! How do they decide which one to pick? And why would they EVER want joe if they could have THIS?* After he felt too full for more, he moved along.

There was a bright, loud store filled with small humans and big humans. Lively music played in the background. At Revver's eye level, he could see interesting, playful things that swirled and turned and made noise. There were other things in colorful boxes. Some of the things had tiny wheels, while some had lights. *Oooh!* Revver ran over to see.

SMACK! Revver ran nose-first into a window! *Ugh! Windows!* he thought once again.

Revver rubbed his cheek with his paw. His face was stinging. *Ouch!* When he looked in again, he saw that some of the small humans inside the store were pointing at him. Their mouths hung open, and they looked surprised and *very amused* to see a squirrel in the airport!

Then Revver looked UP to see a *very large* human standing next to a BIG garbage can on wheels. The human was wearing a green uniform. They did NOT look amused. They did NOT look happy to see Revver.

THEN Revver saw it: the human held **A. Very. Large. STICK**! The stick had a black, brushy end that looked dangerous! Revver gasped and squealed . . . *It's a STICK SHAKER!*

The stick went up into the air and took aim—at Revver's head!

Revver dodged, just in time! The stick barely missed him and *bashed!* onto the ground!

Suddenly, another Stick Shaker appeared. Now two of them were raising their brushy sticks, trying to clobber Revver! Revver started running for his life. The two Stick Shakers left their garbage cans behind and gave chase.

Right up ahead, a third Stick Shaker was waiting, focused on Revver, scowling, with their stick raised high. Revver leaped, flattened himself, and skidded—right between their legs. The Stick

Shaker spun and fell. The two other Stick Shakers fell on top of the first.

Revver looked back over his shoulder but did not stop running. He raced down the long aisle, hiding himself along the edges. He ran straight; he took turns to the right and then left and then ran some more until he felt like he'd gone a very long way. When he finally looked back, he could not see the Stick Shakers anywhere.

Revver was nearing the end of a hallway. To his left, he saw a small, silver metal room. He jumped in to hide and crouched in the corner and panted. For the moment, he felt safe. *Whew! That was close!* He let out a sigh of relief.

In front of him, two doors magically slid out from either side of the front wall—and closed! Revver was shut inside the room! Revver waited, and the strange room started to move! Revver looked up to see lights and buttons but did not know what kind of room—or machine—this might be. It all happened so quickly that Revver didn't even have time to be afraid. This was such a curious thing!

When the doors opened, Revver was in a different place. *Where did it take me? Am I still at the airport?* He crept low and carefully exited the metal room. He stayed near the walls to try to remain hidden.

Then Revver saw the most amazing thing! *Is it some kind of . . . track? A ride, like the shuttle or the moving floor—but just my size?!* Revver watched. A black track moved along, curving and winding its way around the room. Nearby were other tracks, doing the same thing. *Fascinating!*

Some of the tracks were filled with boxes and bags on wheels. Others were empty or mostly empty. *What ARE* **these**? Revver wondered.

He watched the moving tracks. Then he spotted a place—a perfect, squirrel-size place—behind a bag on wheels. Without any thought, he jumped

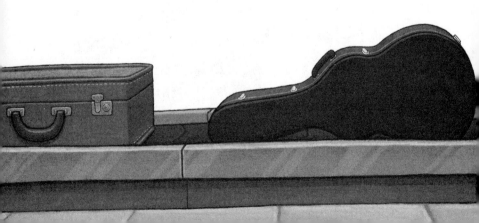

on for a ride! *Now **this** is an adventure!* Revver was giddy. He rode along the twists and turns of the track, hidden by the bag on wheels. The ride was not terribly fast, but it was *always* fun to be riding *something!* He looked at the lights overhead; he peeked out from behind the bag to see people walking and standing. He saw a human's hand reach out. The hand almost took the bag that was hiding Revver. Revver held his breath, but then the hand backed away. *They must have decided they don't want this one,* Revver thought with relief.

Then Revver rode the track into a tunnel. Other bags were put onto the track around him. When he came out of the tunnel, there was a steep downhill where he felt a little speed, and then he was back at the beginning of the ride.

He watched the other tracks. When he was sure he would not be seen, he jumped over and tried them all. The center one was the biggest and his favorite—it had the biggest drop after the tunnel and gave him the most speed!

After a few close calls, he learned quickly to hide behind bags that had gone around the track a few times. It seemed like no one wanted the bags that had been on the ride too long.

He learned that he could ride sitting down or standing up, facing forward or backward. Standing felt more dangerous—so it was more fun! After a few times around, he could ride on one back paw the entire way!

He decided he needed to challenge himself. *I wonder if I could go all the way around, **upside down**.* Revver set his two front paws on the track. It took a few tries, but he finally mastered it perfectly! He went around TWICE in a paw-stand!

Sprite would be so proud of me if she saw this! Revver thought with excitement. Sprite was the nimble, graceful acrobat of the family.

But the thought of his sister made him feel like he'd been *zapped by an electric wire* (which *had* happened a time or two). Revver's mind started racing. His thoughts flew back to his treasured orange chain. And Lou! And Bill! And gate E14!

Revver jumped off the track and tried to remember where he had started. He could feel his heart beating in his ears, and he was shaking. *How long have I been gone?! And **how do I get back**?!*

20

Revver raced around the track room from end to end. He needed to find his way back, but he could not remember where the metal room was! *I need to get back into the metal room!*

He was starting to feel scared—the same kind of scared he'd felt when he could not find Joe. The kind of scared he'd felt when he tried to imagine being **out!** of the team. He was running in circles. His brain was swirling. At last, he tucked into a corner and buried his face in his hands. He felt hopeless. He felt like crying.

Stop and think. It was as if the note magically floated down to him. *My brain burrow! There HAS to be something in there to help me!* Revver shuffled through the pile of ideas and important thoughts he'd collected. Nothing about toilets or tailpipes would help him now; he put all those aside. He found No Pooping in the Garage, and it made him smile for the tiniest moment, remembering that he once did not know that! Then he uncovered Everything Is Connected to Everything Else. He studied and thought about that. He had gotten here. He had found his way *here*. Then he found Be More Patient. He felt ashamed. He knew how he'd gotten himself into this mess. But he would be more patient about finding his way back. And he would never NOT be patient in the crate again. *I can do this*, he promised himself. *I will get back to Bill and the team so we can all go to Charlotte together.*

Revver thought long and hard about how he'd gotten here. He retraced his steps. What had he seen when he left the metal room? He remembered! *There was a table with a human behind it, and there was a picture of a car on the table!*

Now Revver was patient. He looked around. At last, he saw the table and the picture of the car. He turned around, but there was no metal room—only a metal wall. How could this be? He was confused. He stared at the metal wall, trying to make sense of it. Then suddenly . . . it opened!

Some humans walked out of the little metal room, carrying bags and pulling boxes on wheels. Revver stayed off to the side until they passed, and then he ran inside. *How do I make it work?* He pleaded, *Please go . . .* **Please!** Again, the doors magically closed, and he felt the room moving.

When the doors opened, he was back to the aisle where the Stick Shakers had chased him. *I need to find Gate E14.* He'd made so many twists and turns while he was running away, he wasn't sure which way to go. Then something caught his nose. He lifted his nose into the air for a closer smell. He smelled steaming joe. And pizza and tacos and nuts and—*ick! Doughnuts* . . . And instantly, Revver knew how to find his way back!

The smells! They're all **connected** *to E14! I just need to* **smell** *my way back!*

Slowly and patiently, Revver let the smells lead him back to where he had started. He almost paused where he'd tasted the cold, colorful drops, but he stopped himself from going in. *No! I have to get back to Bill and E14!*

Finally, Revver knew—*it's right there! Right around the corner.* He leaped into the room where he had left his crate and Bill—and the chain from Sprite. He bounded in, gleeful! *Yesss! I did it!* He felt victorious!

But his heart quickly sank: Bill and the crew and Revver's crate and Lou and almost everyone else—were gone.

21

Revver went back out and looked around. He came back in. *I'm sure this is the right place.* He double-checked. He triple-checked. He left again and came back again.

Finally, he sat in a corner to think this over. *Could* he be mistaken? Everything did look very much the same.

His world started whirling. Revver plopped down in a corner to try to collect his thoughts. He put his head down into his paws and took a deep breath when he felt something flutter against his foot. He opened his eyes to see a little sparrow, standing beside him.

"Excuse me, are you all right?"

"I'm not exactly sure."

"Perhaps I can help?"

Revver looked closely at the sparrow and thought about what Lucky had told him about birds knowing things. Finally, Revver asked, "Is this gate E14?"

"Yes. Indeed, it is."

"Do you know what happened to the plane to Charlotte?"

"Normally, I would. But the flights have been a mess today because of the storm. I'd recommend that you check with a gate agent."

"I don't know what that is."

"See? Those humans over there." With one wing, the sparrow gestured to two humans in dark-purple uniforms, standing behind a desk.

"Do they speak Squirrel?"

"Highly unlikely."

"So how will I . . . ?" Revver was confused.

"Just stay nearby, where you can hear. You'll learn what you need to know."

Revver stared at the sparrow. Then he turned and studied the humans. He decided to head over there. He turned back to the sparrow. "Okay. Thank y . . . ," he started to say.

But the sparrow was gone.

Revver looked around, but there was no sign of the bird. *Strange.* He shrugged and moved closer to the desk and huddled under a chair to hide.

As he sat, he saw a human walk up to the desk. He could not clearly hear what the human asked. He peeked up from under the chair and saw the uniform person looking at a screen. Then the human with the screen said, very clearly, "Yes, that will be boarding from here, E14. The earlier scheduled flight to Charlotte just departed."

Revver gasped. *Departed? DEPARTED?!* **It LEFT?!** *Without me?!*

Revver forgot all about staying near the walls and avoiding the Stick Shakers. He ran to the window at the back of the room and saw a plane rolling away. If only he could jump out, he could get to that plane! He could make them stop for him! Instead, he pressed his whole self against the window, only able to watch.

That was another problem with windows.

Now Revver was stuck here, looking at the plane—the plane that held Bill with Revver's empty crate, and the rest of the team, and Lou, with his treasured chain from Sprite.

Revver watched, stunned, as the plane slowly began to move.

22

For a long time, Revver stood at the window. He didn't move or blink. He wasn't sure he even took a breath.

He watched the plane get in line behind another plane, and wait for its turn to take off. He stared helplessly as the plane gathered speed and raised its nose and took off into the sky. If he were in a different mood, he would find this incredible and exciting. Now, it made him feel like he was seeing all his happiness fly away.

He kept watching the plane—the plane that carried Bill and the crew to Charlotte. He watched until he could no longer see it, until it disappeared high into the sky.

Then he just kept standing there, pressed against the glass. Time passed. The skies darkened; Revver was not sure if it was because it was nighttime or if another rainstorm might be coming. It didn't matter. He didn't care.

After a long, long time, he peeled himself away from the window. He dropped his head and began to walk. He didn't know where.

He walked past all the places he had explored earlier—all the places he had found so interesting and exciting. Now he did not even bother to look up.

His mind flashed bits and pieces of memories—of his time with the team, with Bill. He remembered his first ride in a race car and the feeling of pure speed—and pure joy. He remembered wiring cars and fetching tools and holding things when he was asked. He loved helping. He remembered Susan patiently teaching him wiring. He remembered watching Bill practice his tire changing while Revver fetched lug nuts for him. "Bill. Bill. Bill." Revver mumbled Bill's name.

He remembered all the hours riding in the truck with Joe, looking out the windows and munching peanuts and listening to the radio while they rolled along. He remembered the fluffy shop towels and how everyone rubbed him behind the ears.

He remembered all the sights and feelings and smells of the garage, the cars, and the track. He remembered how Ashley always smelled flowery and how Trevor sometimes had a strong smell that made Bill say, "Dude, you swimmin' in aftershave again?" He knew the smells of rubber and fuel and exhaust. He remembered the life, where everyone loved cars and speed and racing as much as he did—where he felt loved and *understood*.

He remembered the horrible smell of the "joe" that Joe drank, and he even missed that.

But again and again, he thought of Bill. Thinking of Bill made a lump form in the bottom of Revver's throat. Bill was his best friend, his favorite human in the whole world. Revver loved the whole crew, but mostly, he loved Bill.

Revver somehow found himself down by the tracks where he'd been playing earlier. He remembered feeling so giddy then. *I was having so much fun.* He sighed, sadly realizing that he was probably playing there when everyone got on the plane—without him.

Straight ahead, large glass doors were sliding open and closed. Revver could feel a blast of warm, humid air when they opened.

Without even thinking about it, he went outside.

23

Even the sounds of horns and whistles and squealing tires and people yelling and feet running did not break Revver's thoughts. He just kept walking along the hard, hot concrete. He had no idea where he was going.

It started to rain again. *I hate rain*, Revver thought. He didn't even have enough energy left in him to be angry. He just lowered his head even farther, trying to tuck his face into his chest, and kept walking.

It rained harder. Revver remembered what Lucky had said: *There is nothing more pathetic than a wet mouse.* He felt the rain running off his back as he trudged, ankle-deep in water. *Pathetic*. Now Revver understood the word—because that's exactly how he felt.

Cars screeched and roared by. More horns honked. Revver smelled exhaust from cars coming *very* close, but he did not care. He paid no attention; he had no destination in mind. He just kept walking.

After a while, the rain stopped. He noticed that now he was walking on cool, wet grass. He didn't know how he'd gotten there, but he stopped and looked up. Revver was in the middle of a long, large island of grass and trees. He could see lanes of cars moving on either side of the island. To his left, cars were moving one way. To his right, cars were moving in the other direction.

For the first time since he left the window of gate E14, Revver stopped walking. He found a spot under a tree and plopped down. There was something about the tree that felt comforting. It felt good to rest.

"Hi!" A chipper voice startled Revver.

Revver heard the word but could not see who had said it. "Um. Hello?" he answered.

"What brings you here?! Are you . . . *lost?!*"

"No. I mean, yes. Or I guess so. I mean, I don't know where I should go or what I should do."

Above Revver's head, he heard leaves rustling. Soon, a squirrel appeared. It ran down the tree trunk and sat across from Revver.

This squirrel was not brown, like the squirrels Revver knew. This squirrel was gray and almost exactly Revver's size.

"So what brings you *here?*" This new squirrel seemed very excited.

"Where is *here?*" Revver asked.

"Here. In Median."

"What's *Median?*"

"It's not a *what*; it's a *where*, silly! And *here* you are!"

"In Median."

"Exactly!"

Revver said nothing but studied this new

126

squirrel for a moment. The squirrel was smiling. She had big, bright eyes and seemed very happy.

"We don't get many visitors here. It's just *awfully* nice to see a new face! Visitors sometimes TRY to get here, you know, but, *well . . .*" The new squirrel pointed to the rows of traffic on either side of them. "It mostly does not end well. But you, YOU made it here! *How wonderful!*"

As the squirrel spoke, a bluebird flew in from a nearby tree and sat next to them. "And who is your new friend?" the bird asked.

"Well, I don't know yet! I was just about to ask!"

Revver just sat, looking from the squirrel to the bird and back again.

"*Well?*" asked the squirrel, a little impatient.

"Well, *what?*" Revver was confused.

"What's your name, *silly!*"

"Oh." Revver paused a moment. "Revver. My name is Revver."

"Ooooh. I've never met ANYONE with that name. *It's so interesting!* Why did your mama name you *that?*"

"Well, um . . ." Revver's mind was jumbled. He tried to find the words he wanted. "It's because of a loud sound I make. When I'm very excited, I mean. Or very happy." Revver sighed. He was pretty sure he'd never feel happy again.

"Oh! That's *wonderful*! Can *we* hear it?"

"Hear what?"

"The sound you make, of course!"

"Oh. Probably not."

"But why?"

"Because I don't feel very excited right now. Or happy."

"You're not happy?! Oh, that's SO SAD! I'm almost always happy! That's why I'm GLEE! I mean, Hello, Revver! My name is Glee! It's ever so nice to meet you!"

Revver could almost have guessed her name. She was bursting with joyful energy.

"So why, *why* aren't you happy, Revver?" Both the squirrel and the bird looked *extremely* interested. The squirrel continued. "I promise, it's *very* nice here in Median. And look at all these NUT TREES! This is a *wonderful* place to live!"

"I concur," said the bluebird. "I, of course, am free to travel about. But I always come back to Median! It's so lovely. Nice and peaceful. Although, I guess it CAN get a bit boring."

"Which is why we're so happy that someone new has come to live here!"

"But I don't WANT to live here. I want to get to *Charlotte*."

"Oooo-ooooh," said the bluebird.

"Ohhhhhhh!" said Glee.

The squirrel and the bluebird seemed excited. They looked at each other as if they had a wonderful new secret. Revver looked back and forth between both of them.

Finally, Glee spoke. "And *who*, may we ask, is *Charrrrrrlotte?*" Now she was nearly face-to-face with Revver, and her eyes were wide and excited. She said *Charlotte* in the strangest, most dramatic way.

Revver was confused again.

Then the bluebird said, "Perhaps Charlotte is your *girlfrrrriend*?" The last word sounded like a song.

"My gir . . . ? No, wait. No. What?! **No!!!**"

"Well, then *who* is she?" the bluebird asked, tilting his head to show that this was VERY interesting.

"She's not . . . No. Stop. Not a SHE. I mean, it's not a **who**; it's a **where**. *Charlotte* is a PLACE."

"Oh. Well." Glee sighed a long, disappointed sigh. She moved away from Revver and plopped down on the ground. "That's just not *nearly* as exciting to talk about, right, Blue?"

The bluebird agreed. "Not as exciting *at all*."

"What's exciting?! *What's* exciting?!" A chipmunk had leaped in out of nowhere and joined the group.

"Revver wants to get to Charlotte."

"Oh! How wonderful!!! What's a *Revver*?"

"It's not a *what*; it's a *who*."

"THIS is Revver," said the gray squirrel, pointing at Revver.

"Oh! A new friend! That IS exciting! Well, then who is Charlotte, *hmmmmm?!*" Like the others, the chipmunk seemed way too interested.

All together, Revver, the gray squirrel, and the bluebird said, "It's not a *who*; it's a *where!*"

"Oh. Well, darn. That's not nearly as exciting."

"Yeah, yeah," whistled the bluebird. "We were just saying that."

"I'm so tired," said Revver. "I've had the longest day. A terrible, longest day."

"Oh!!! That sounds like a *wonderful, exciting* story! Please, Revver, tell us a story."

"We DO love a good story."

"And it's so dull here sometimes. We would love to hear about something *exciting!*"

"Yes, please, Revver—*please* tell us about your longest, terrible-est day."

The squirrel, the bluebird, and the chipmunk crowded around. They all sat together, in a circle, under the tree, looking at Revver.

Revver sighed. "It's just that . . . Well . . . I've been in the airport for a long, long time."

"The AIRPORT!"

"NO! You were IN the airport?! Please tell us about that!"

"We love hearing about what goes on in the airport!"

"We've heard many stories, *of course*, but you never *really* know what to believe."

"The birds have told us *a few* things . . ."

"Oh, *yes*, Revver! *Please* tell us about the airport and your terrible-est day."

24

Revver had not been able to talk—really talk—to anyone since he had left his family in the grove and joined the race team. Bill and the crew were pretty good at understanding what Revver wanted or needed, but it was different to be able to *actually* talk to someone and have them understand you. Or some*ones*, in this case. His heart was so heavy, he felt like he *needed* to talk.

Where can I even begin? Revver thought. He looked at his eager audience as they all sat, anxious to hear his story. He settled back against the tree to get comfortable and cleared his throat. He tried hard to organize his thoughts, which was not easy after his terrible-est day. He checked through

133

his brain burrow notes, trying to remember all he'd learned. Then he began at the beginning—in the nest.

Glee and Chipmunk and Blue were spellbound by Revver's story. When he got to the part about saving his family from the hawk, Revver's fur-and-feather audience cheered. When he told about Sprite being trapped in a deep hole guarded by coyotes, the three of them did not blink or move. They waited in suspense to see how that part of the story would end. They booed Grumpy Jack. They cheered when the race team won! They laughed at Revver's ride on the sunglasses tower. They screamed when the car hauler hit the long black limo and Revver saw that it was Jack lying on the ground.

When Revver got to the part about the airport, he tried to remember every single detail, because his new friends wanted to know everything.

"*Fascinating!*" they said again and again.

Then he told them about what had happened with Lou.

"Oh! That *awful* cat! That's terrible!"

"Horrible! What a *nasty*, NASTY thing to do!"

"Wait," Revver said, trying to understand what they were saying, "you think Lou did that to me *on purpose*? You think he *wanted* me to miss the plane?"

"Absolutely."

"Not a doubt."

"My mother said that you can NEVER, EVER trust a cat!" said Chipmunk.

"SOOO true!" said Blue. "I could tell *you* some tales of the cats I've known and heard about . . ." Blue stopped, eager for Revver to continue.

It took a long, long time but, at last, Revver finished his story. "And that's how I ended up here, with you."

Revver let out a long, deep exhale. He rubbed his eyes with his paws and then put his face into his hands. He was completely exhausted. He looked up and realized that it was dark. *How long was I in the airport? How long have I* **been** *here?* He didn't know.

No one spoke. Finally, Glee asked, "So, Revver, what are you going to *do?*"

"I just don't know. I'm so awfully tired." He tried to remember how this had all started, back at the track, before the airport. That seemed like a long, long time ago. "I guess I'll just stay *here.*" Revver said *here* like he was about to eat something horrible.

"Oh! That would be *wonderful!*" Chipmunk shouted out and jumped and clapped his paws together. But Blue and Glee shook their heads.

"*Oh, Revver.* You can't stay here. You would never be happy. It's pleasant and peaceful in Median, but it's *not at all* fast or exciting." Something about the way Glee said that reminded Revver so much of Sprite. The thought of his sister made him ache even more. He looked down at his ankle, where the braided cord had been.

"Well . . . YOU like it here," Revver said, looking around at all of them.

"But WE only like *excitement* . . ." Glee searched for a way to explain it . . .

"From the sidelines!" Chipmunk chimed in.

"Exactly!" Glee said.

Revver thought about this. "Like . . . the people watching the race from the stands?"

"Indeed. Very much like *that*," said Blue.

Revver was quiet.

Glee looked Revver in the eyes. "But YOU, you *love* speed and excitement! It's what makes you happy! That's why you have to GO, Revver. Your place is with Bill and the team. You have to try to get home."

Once, Sprite had said almost this exact thing to Revver. His thoughts swirled from the grove to Median . . . to Bill.

Now, Glee was right. Revver wanted desperately to go home. And *home*, he knew, was with Bill.

"I have . . . nowhere else to go." Revver's eyes were heavy. "Nowhere," he said again, softly.

"Here, Revver," Glee said. She grabbed his wrist gently and led him around to the other side of the tree trunk. "Why don't you rest? In this little cavity, right here." She pointed to a little hollow in the tree, near the ground.

Once again, Glee reminded Revver of his sister. Sprite always tried to take care of him.

"See?" Glee gently nudged him into the cavity. "You need some sleep. You'll be warm and covered here, in case it rains."

"I really hate rain," Revver mumbled. But he was already half asleep as he crawled into the burrow.

"Good night, Revver," Glee said as she shimmied up the tree to her own bed.

Swooshhh. Swooshhh. Swooshhh. Glee settled down to sleep to the sound of cars going by on the wet streets, on either side of the little forest. But every once in a while, she could hear Revver crying out in his sleep. "Bill! *Where are you? Why,* **WHY** *didn't I just stay in the crate?!*"

25

"Revver!" Something was tapping on his shoulder. "Revver!" *Tap-tap-tap!* He had never heard someone yell and whisper at the same time.

Revver forced open his eyes and saw Chipmunk, Blue, and Glee standing in front of the hollow. The sun was up. Glee had been prodding him awake.

When he remembered where he was, all the horrible facts came back to him. *How long have I been asleep?* Revver didn't know. He sat up, but he felt so heavy. There was a little pile of nuts in front of him that someone had gathered. But he didn't feel like eating.

"We need a plan," Glee said. The other two nodded energetically.

"What kind of plan?"

"A plan to get you to Charlotte."

"But . . . *how?*"

"Well, we don't exactly have that figured out yet."

"That's why we need a plan, *silly!*"

"We've been awake for *hours*, discussing it."

"You *have?*" Revver was still groggy.

"Of course."

"But . . . *why?*"

"Because we want to help you."

"But . . . you barely know me. Why do you want to help me?"

"Because you're our *friend!*" Glee made this sound obvious.

"I am?"

"Of course you are!" Chipmunk piped up.

"Plus, it's the circle!"

Revver looked around at the others, trying to clear the fog from his tired brain as Blue nodded to assure him. Revver did not know what *the circle* meant, but Blue interrupted his thoughts.

"Now, back to work." Blue sounded serious. "We need to focus on a *plan*."

"You could walk to Charlotte!" Glee shouted.

"*I could?* How long would that take?"

"I predict . . ." Blue closed his eyes and whistled. He tipped his head to one side. "Approximately eighty-seven hours. About four days."

"But if you *run*, you could probably make it in two days!"

"Hmm." Blue was whistling again. "But that is by the most direct route, which means the highways. Not recommended."

"Ah. So true."

Blue hummed and thought. "So let's assummme—about a week. Provided he has a good sense of direction. And, of course, also provided that he doesn't stop."

"How do you *know* all of this?" Revver asked.

Glee piped up. "Birds know *everything*."

Revver remembered what Lucky had told him.

141

"Plus, he'd have to get through there." Glee pointed to the traffic on either side. It would be a challenge.

"Definitely. But *not* impossible."

"We *have* seen it happen a time or two," Chipmunk said, excited.

"Of course, but there have been SO MANY *other* times . . ."

"Even if I *could* get through the traffic"—Revver looked at the cars rushing by on either side and shuddered when he thought about those *other times*—"I don't want to walk—or run—for an entire week!"

"Without stopping."

Revver ignored that. It was ridiculous. He went on. "Plus, even if I DID get there in a week, the race in Charlotte would be over by then, and the team would already be heading to the *next* race."

"Where is the next race—after Charlotte?"

Revver sighed. "I dunno."

"Idaho?!" Blue jumped back, alarmed.

"Idaho is very, VERY far away!"

"But I HAVE heard it's lovely."

"No!" Revver did not even know what Idaho was. "I said, *I. Don't. Know!*"

"Oh, well that's an entirely different matter altogether."

Revver rolled his eyes. He shook his head and put his face in his paws. He sighed again, a long, deep, hopeless sigh.

This was not feeling promising.

26

By late morning, it felt like every option had been discussed.

"It's simple. Just go back into the airport and take the next plane to Charlotte!" Chipmunk had a lot of ideas.

The thought made Revver shiver. He tried to imagine getting past security, trying to find the gate, all alone, trying not to be seen by anyone—especially the Stick Shakers. "I—I—I just don't think I could do that by myself."

"It *does* sound rather complicated."

"You could climb over the fence BEHIND the airport and sneak in UNDER the plane—with all the bags!" squealed Chipmunk.

"How would he know which plane was the *right* plane? He could end up ANYWHERE."

"I didn't think of that."

"How about, we could *mail* him? We'd just need a box. And lots of tape. And an address. And then we would need to find a place to . . ."

Once Blue explained exactly how MAIL worked, it seemed like a terribly complicated idea.

"A boat!"

"Impossible. No rivers between here and there."

"Any oceans?"

"Not a one." Blue shook his head.

"You could DRIVE with someone . . ."

"Yes! Like Joe!"

"Joe left yesterday." Revver chimed in here.

"Someone else in this city HAS to be driving from here to Charlotte."

"I'm certain of that," said Blue. "But in our position, finding a human who would agree to drive a squirrel to Charlotte is not terribly realistic."

"Couldn't you just pick him up and fly him there?"

"Chipmunk! Look at the size of Revver and look at the size of Blue! How could he possibly . . ."

"Quite true," said Blue, "although I DO have a hawk friend who would be quite excited to take on the challenge!" The bird chuckled at his own joke. Everyone knew that hawks and squirrels (and chipmunks, for that matter) were a *deadly* combination.

"That's a horrible joke." Chipmunk pouted.

No one else found it funny, either.

"Yes, of course." Blue cleared his throat. "Sorry. Just a bit of bird humor to try to lighten the mood."

Everyone sat quietly thinking. Revver picked at a few of the nuts they had brought him. Time passed.

"I do have one idea. Although it's quite complicated. But I believe . . . I believe that it might be our only hope."

Revver sat up straight. Glee and Chipmunk perked to attention.

Blue closed his eyes and tilted his head. He whistled, allowing his thoughts to come together.

"Yes," he said at last. "I believe it can work. It won't be easy. It DEFINITELY won't be easy . . . but I really see no other way."

Again, Blue was quietly whistling. "It will take some luck." He whistled some more. "And he'll need my help, of course."

"Well, of course, Blue!" Glee was excited, even though she had no idea what the plan might be.

Blue said, finally, "There's a train. It's a long and dangerous road to get to the station. BUT if we can make it, it goes straight to Charlotte from here."

"Ohhh! A TRAIN!" Glee burst out.

The bird continued. "It leaves tonight. Revver, you'll need to be on that train to have any chance of getting to the race."

27

"FIRST," Blue continued, "you'll need to get out of Median." The group glanced at the lanes of traffic rushing by on their left and right, three lanes of speeding cars on each side.

"Revver, how did you get in here in the first place? YOU made it through."

"I'm not really sure. I left the airport and just started walking . . . I wasn't paying attention."

"We're going to just call that luck. Or fate."

"Oh, yes! Fate! That sounds so exciting! FATE brought Revver here!"

Blue rolled his eyes. "I'd like him to be a little more careful on the way back through. We don't want to 'tempt fate'—as they say."

Three of them nodded in agreement.

"What's FATE?" Revver asked.

Glee piped up. "It's when something happens because it is *just meant to be*."

"Like you getting to Median."

"And meeting us!"

"So we can help you."

"Oh," Revver said. He wasn't really convinced that FATE was on his side at the moment.

Blue cleared his throat to get them back to business. "And then there's the matter of getting from here, the airport, to the train station. That's about fifteen miles. It's a bit to the east but mostly north. According to my math, that will take about three hours, at a good, steady squirrel pace."

"I can do that," Revver said, trying to sound confident. But Revver had never tried to keep moving for three entire hours. He actually wasn't sure.

"I'll fly overhead to lead you. But we're going to need to go alongside the highway. It's dangerous, but it's the most direct route. There's no time for anything else.

"And then there's the matter of getting you ON the train. We're just going to have to deal with that when we get there.

"Finally, when you arrive in Charlotte, you're going to have to get from *that* train station to the speedway. According to my sources, that will be about another fifteen miles. I won't be there to help you with that. You'll have to figure it out on your own."

Revver nodded, barely, trying to picture it all in his mind. It was very complicated, but it was his only chance to find Bill.

"So! **All *he* needs to do is** get across three lanes of traffic, make his way to the highway, keep a steady pace along the interstate road for about three hours—*without* getting hit by a car, of course—get to the train station, get onto the train, get to Charlotte, get off the train, and find his way to the track! Easy peasy!" Glee clapped her paws joyfully. She had said *all of that* without taking a single breath of air.

Blue was very serious. He looked squarely at Revver. "Do you think you can do all that?"

Moments passed.

"Revver, it's important that you understand: there will be no time for mistakes. No time to waste. Everything will need to go exactly right. You. Cannot. Miss. That. Train."

Blue, Glee, and Chipmunk sat looking at Revver. They waited.

At last, Revver said, "When do we leave?"

"Immediately."

28

"I wish there was something . . . something I could *give* you . . . to *repay* you."

"Repay us?!"

"For *what*?"

"Yes, *why on earth* would you need to PAY us?"

"Because . . . well, because you have all done so much. You've been so . . . *nice*."

"Oh, Revver. That's not how it works!"

"Not how *what* works?"

"The circle!"

"The circle?"

"Of course!"

Revver still had no idea what this meant. Once

again, Blue interrupted his thoughts before he could ask questions.

"True, true," Blue chimed in, "no payment is expected or required, friend. Now, we really must get *on* with it."

There wasn't much time for goodbyes. Before he knew it, Revver was standing at the edge of Median, waiting for the right moment to cross three lanes of speeding cars. Blue had already flown over and was waiting for him on the other side. Glee and Chipmunk watched from behind him. He knew they were scared. HE was scared!

Revver took a deep breath and seized a moment. He darted out to cross. But he instantly questioned himself. WAS that the right time to go? WAS there enough time to get across? He hesitated. He was in the middle of the center lane when he looked to his left to see a front bumper heading right toward him. He panicked! He froze!

He could hear Glee screaming! At the very last moment, he realized what he'd done. He dropped and flattened himself on the road. The car zoomed over him. And then another car. And another. He could hear Glee crying out his name.

To the others, Revver most certainly looked dead.

Revver's heart was pounding. He remembered what his mother had said about cars in Squirrel School. *If you get near that, you'll end up flat!* He did NOT want to end up flat. He decided, *THIS is NOT how it's going to end!* His thoughts were swirling around. *Think! Think!* He begged himself, *THINK! You can't stay HERE!*

He lifted up his head just enough for his eyes to see what was coming. Finally, his instincts started to come back. He began talking to himself. "You KNOW cars. You *know* how to do this. Just like the track. Think like a driver. Find the right moment to get through." Something clicked in him. It was the most normal he'd felt since he first went into the crate.

Now he saw everything in slow motion: as soon as a car passed over him and he saw a space, he jumped to his feet! He dashed and made it across the middle lane! He waited on the line separating the middle lane from the last lane. Cars raced by behind him; there was a strong breeze from them against his back; he had to force his feet to stay planted on the ground so he didn't blow forward.

He saw a gap in the cars, and, with all his might, he pounced across the third lane to safety. For the first time in a very long time, he felt so happy, he roared, *"Vr-vr-vr-VRRROOOOM!"*

He caught his breath. He turned and looked back across the three lanes of traffic. Among the cars, he could see Glee and Chipmunk standing and watching, stunned. Glee had her paws over her mouth.

I made it! he thought. He felt giddy! Revver waved and yelled, "That was a present for you! I wanted to give you something *exciting* to see!"

In the gaps among the cars, Revver waved at them one last time. He saw them wave back, and he could see they were happy. Then he turned away. He knew he still had a long, long way to go.

Blue was sitting just ahead. "Well now, we're off to the highway. I'll fly above and ahead to lead you. Oh, and I'd prefer a little less *drama* along the way, if you don't mind."

29

Getting to the highway was no easy task. Blue guided the way from above while Revver kept a steady pace, looking up at Blue to make sure he was on track.

Blue sat on a nearby tree or electric line and waited when Revver was delayed—waiting for cars to pass by or having to wind his way around obstacles.

Once in a while, Blue would shout out, "A little faster, please, Revver. Time is ticking."

Every time Blue said it, Revver would imagine missing the train—watching it in the distance, just like the plane he had missed. The thought jolted him, and he ran faster.

The route took Revver through two huge parking lots (dangerously close to some cars backing up), a park (with a yappy dog who chased Revver up a tree), and across several small roads. It also required that Revver travel around a garbage dump—which smelled absolutely horrible. Revver decided that his brother Farty's butt stink smelled like flowers compared to this.

Around the dump, Revver tried breathing through his mouth instead of his nose—to avoid *smelling*. But he kept sucking in flies. *Ugh!* He spit them out every time. He looked up to see that Blue was flying much higher to avoid the stench.

Revver was starting to get in a bad mood. He tried to remind himself that it was his own fault he'd gotten in this whole mess in the first place. *If only I'd stayed in the crate. If I had just been more patient . . .* He pushed on.

FINALLY, they arrived at the entrance to the highway.

Revver had seen many highways. In the hauler

with Joe, they covered miles and miles of busy roads and interstates. But when Revver drove along with Joe, he sat in a comfortable seat, on his fluffy towel, with air-conditioning, the radio, snacks, and Joe to keep him company.

The highway looked very different from the ground. It was a sizzling afternoon. He could feel the heat of the road—and he could actually *see* it, in blurry waves rising from the street. He could feel the dust and exhaust trailing behind the cars and trucks. The hot fumes blew into his face each time a car went by.

Blue flew down to the ground and stood in front of Revver.

"Only about thirteen miles left now. Stay on the side, on the shoulder of the road, as far away from the traffic as you can. But try to keep clear of the ditch; it's steep, and the weeds are high. It will slow you down, and there is no time to slow down." Blue kept talking. "Oh, and the off-ramps and on-ramps will take some thinking. You'll have to climb around and over those and then get back on the route. Okay?"

"I guess," Revver said, hoping he remembered everything. He was nervous. He was also *already* hot and tired.

"If we keep a good pace, you'll be at the train station just in time."

Revver nodded.

"Good, let's get going, then." Blue flew up and ahead. "And by the way, you smell really terrible." The odor from the dump was stuck on Revver.

"Great."

"Hopefully, you'll air out on the way."

"Hopefully."

As he scampered along, Revver noticed some curious things about the highway. He saw SO MANY abandoned shoes. Never a pair. Always just one. Why always just ONE shoe? He tried to imagine what would make a human toss a shoe out of a moving car or stop their car to remove a shoe and throw it away.

He saw other things, too: long black skid marks from someone hitting their brakes too fast and hard. He imagined some of the high-speed near misses he'd seen at the track.

He saw empty cans and cups and bottles. Sometimes a shirt or a sock—or pants. Then, a sink. And farther up, an entire couch! To entertain himself, he tried to make up stories about how these things might have ended up on the road. This gave Revver something to think about for a while and took his mind off things for a few miles. *Humans are just so ODD*, he decided.

His thoughts were regularly broken by Blue ordering him to go faster or by horns honking or loud music from a passing car.

Thud! Revver, startled, was almost hit in the face by a white bag full of garbage that smelled like french fries. A split second later, a cup flew from the same car, throwing something dark and

sticky all over him. He tried to shake off the wet-
ness and keep moving. Now all the dust, dirt, and
gravel from the road were sticking to him.

How rude! Revver thought. *Joe would **never**
do anything like that!* Right away, he pushed the
thought of Joe and the truck out of his mind. It
reminded him how miserable he was. And it made
him miss his racing family too much. He couldn't
let himself think about how afraid he was—afraid
of the journey but more afraid that he wouldn't
make it to them in time.

30

Revver smelled it before he saw it. Something furry and FLAT—he didn't look too closely—was on the road. He heard the chanting in his memory, *If you get near that, you'll end up **FLAT***. Revver shuddered, reminding himself to stay far off to the side and to keep paying attention. He took a long circle around *the something*, but it reminded him how dangerous this all was.

Every time a car passed, he got another face full of exhaust. After the first few miles, Revver's paws were getting sore from the hot road and all the bits of gravel along the shoulder. He grew grumpier.

A few more miles passed. He heard an odd flapping sound behind him, getting louder as it came closer, *plap-plap-plappity-plap!* As a car passed, Revver looked up to see a black blur heading toward him. He didn't duck in time. It hit him across the face, hard. He just stood there, a little stunned, rubbing his stinging face.

"Yowch!" Revver yelled.

"Are you okay?" Blue asked from above.

Revver looked down to find a piece of rubber that had fallen off the tire of a passing car. He angrily tossed the rubber into the ditch. His mood wasn't getting better. "FINE. Let's just keep going!" Revver yelled back.

He ran on, but he was feeling annoyed. Furious, actually. His fur felt stiff and heavy from all the dirt and small rocks that stuck to him after a drink had soaked him. He was *fuming* about all the trash and the flying piece of rubber. His brain was so full of angry thoughts that he wasn't paying attention—and he tripped over an abandoned tailpipe! He flew forward and skidded on his front paws and his belly. The metal tailpipe, which had been baking in the hot sun, burned his ankle on the way down. Revver was there, on his stomach, on the shoulder of the road. His arms and legs were all spread out. He just stayed there, panting and groaning. Now his temper was flaring.

Blue flew right down to check. "Are you okay, Revver?"

Revver did not move.

"*Hmm?*" Blue hummed as he pecked at him lightly. "All okay?"

Finally, Revver stumbled to his feet, which still hurt. His burned ankle also hurt. His stomach and front paws were stinging, all scraped up from falling on the road. His face had a long red mark from the tire rubber slap. He was a hot, sticky, dirty, matted, ANGRY mess.

"All okay?! **ALL OKAY?!** NO, NO, it's NOT okay. It's all AWFUL. It's TERRIBLE. So no, NO, NOOOOO! I am NOT okay!" An angry Revver marched around, stomping hard and throwing his arms into the air.

Just then, a loud **BANG!** then **SCRRREEEECH!** broke the rhythm of Revver's temper tantrum.

Blue jerked and fluttered out of the way, flying into a nearby tree for safety.

Revver dived into the ditch just as a car squealed onto the shoulder, barely missing him. It had lost control. It skidded back and forth, tipped left to right, until it finally rolled to a safe stop, with a popped front tire. There the car sat, lopsided.

At the bottom of the ditch was a small stream. Revver sat in the black water, surrounded by weeds and prickly branches. Now he was scratched up from head to toe and covered with burs. He just sat there. The fear and the water had taken away his anger.

SSS-ssssssssss!

Revver held his breath and then heard it again. **SSS-ssssssssss!**

Revver leaped out of the ditch! He jumped back onto the hot, dusty, gravelly shoulder of the road with his sopping-wet self—just as a long black snake wiggled along the ditch where he had just been sitting.

Blue had returned and now stood in front of him. "Oh, good. I see you're fine. Let's keep on, then. And, Revver, please HURRY. There's no time for any more delays."

Revver sighed. He wasn't angry anymore. The near miss of the car, the fall into the water, and the run-in with the snake snapped him back to remembering why he was here in the first place. He needed to get to Charlotte. He had no choice but to keep going.

Revver got up and scurried forward a few leaps, but he had a nagging feeling. He stopped and looked back at the stalled car with the flat tire. The driver had gotten out of the car and was squatting down on the side of the road, examining the remains of the popped rubber on the rim.

"*The time*, Revver, remember *the time!*" Blue was circling above Revver's head.

The car's windows were now rolled down, and Revver could hear a little human crying inside the car. The nagging feeling got bigger. Revver knew: he could not leave.

31

The driver stood slowly and scratched his head. He moved toward the trunk of the car. Revver moved closer to watch as the driver opened the trunk and looked in. In the background, Blue was chirping about having to move on, but Revver didn't hear him. He was focused on the human.

The driver looked into the trunk of the car for a long while but didn't move. He scratched his head again. Revver found this fascinating. And strange. He had seen dozens of tire changes on the track, all at lightning speed. This human seemed to be moving in slow motion. Or perhaps, not moving AT. ALL. "The only thing worse than *slow* is *stopped*," Revver heard himself say.

The human looked around and saw Revver. Their eyes met. The human shrugged and went back to peering into the trunk. Revver heard the little human inside the car, crying louder now.

This is taking too long! Revver jumped onto the back wheel and onto the side of the open trunk. The human startled, but he didn't move away. He just stared at Revver, unsure of what to think.

Revver noticed that the human was sweating and seemed nervous. Finally, he stopped staring at Revver and went back to staring into the trunk of the car.

Revver peeked in. The trunk was messy, filled with scattered papers and bags. There were some things that Revver guessed belonged to the small human—soft, colorful things.

Revver took the lead. He jumped into the trunk. The human gasped but watched. Revver dug around, shuffling through paper and tossing things out of the way. At last, he found it: *Oh, good! It's here!* He dragged a lug wrench out into the open toward the driver. The driver stared at the lug wrench and then at Revver. Finally, the human dutifully lifted the tool out of the trunk.

Then he crinkled his forehead, shook his head, and ran a hand through his hair. He mumbled something like, "Is this for REAL?" but he kept watching Revver closely.

Next, Revver uncovered the jack. It was too heavy for him to lift, but he pointed it out to the driver by tapping on it with his paw. The driver still seemed a little unsure but was catching on. He lifted the jack.

Revver jumped out of the trunk and onto the shoulder of the road. He tugged on the driver's pants leg, and the man followed Revver to the front tire, carrying the wrench and the jack. Revver waited for the human to get to work, but the driver just stood there, staring blankly at the ruined tire.

Suddenly, a thought hit Revver. *He's never changed a tire before!* Now Revver was excited! He had a chance to teach someone something, after the team had taught HIM *so much!*

"Don't worry! I'll show you!" Revver exclaimed. Of course, the human did not understand Squirrel, but he watched as Revver pointed to the jack and showed him where to position it, to secure it under the frame of the car. Revver indicated how to turn the handle so that the car would lift, and the human followed Revver's directions.

Nearby, Blue stopped urging Revver to keep going. He sat quietly and watched closely.

Revver pointed from the lug wrench to the lug nuts on the tire. The driver's eyes flashed. Revver saw the look and knew what it meant. *It's making sense! He understands! He's learning!* The human nodded and quickly got to work, loosening the lug nuts and setting them aside.

Revver continued instructing the driver. All the while, the man kept whispering under his breath, "No one would believe *this* . . . ," "Changing a tire *with a squirrel* . . . ," "Not even sure this is really happening . . ." But he kept following Revver's directions.

Step-by-step, the old tire was removed. The driver carried a new one from the trunk. Revver put on the lug nuts, and the driver tightened them. Revver checked that the nuts were secure. *All good!* Revver tapped the tire twice and nodded, as best as a squirrel can nod, to let the driver know that he was good to go. Revver lowered the jack to set the car back on the ground.

The driver looked at Revver, his eyes wide and his mouth hanging open in a huge "O."

Revver noticed that it was quiet. He peeked up into the half-open window of the back seat and saw that the small human was asleep.

The driver picked up the old tire and the tools and put them into the trunk. He closed the trunk and looked back around at Revver. "Um . . ." He mumbled something Revver could not understand and then said, "Uhhh, *thanks?*"

Revver nodded again as the driver shook his head in disbelief—then he started the car, rolled up the windows, and drove back onto the highway.

Blue flew closer and asked quietly, "Ready?"

"Ready, Blue," Revver said softly. He leaped forward, back on track. He knew that he had lost valuable time. They might miss the train. He was grateful that Blue did not mention that.

32

Blue flew up and ahead, to guide Revver.

There was still enough light to see the way—but barely. *We've been traveling almost a whole day,* Revver thought. The sky was growing dark, quickly. He felt like he'd said goodbye to Glee and Chipmunk so long ago . . .

After a while, Blue led Revver away from the highway. Revver tried running more quickly. *Maybe I can make up for lost time,* he thought. But he was almost afraid to hope.

Blue directed Revver across a road, then through a small field and through another parking lot.

And there, at long last, was the train station. Revver held his breath.

Everything felt still and quiet. Revver waited and looked.

Suddenly, *ting!-ting!-ting!* It was the most beautiful sound Revver had ever heard! The train was pulling into the station!

Hisssss! The train stopped.

"We haven't missed it! Blue, it's here!" Revver was screaming over the sounds of the train. The air was filled with a strange, electric smell that Revver found *delicious!*

We didn't miss it! We didn't miss it! Revver kept repeating it over and over. Overhead, Blue flapped joyfully.

Revver could see lights inside the train cars. He could see humans here and there, already inside, sitting next to the windows. He could see underneath the train to the other side. When he looked between the cars, he could see how they were attached together. He studied these things a long time, because he always liked to know how things worked. He remembered a note: Everything Is Connected to

Everything Else. That was definitely true with trains.

Revver and Blue hid, watching. They could see a human in a uniform standing in front of the stairs to the train. Other humans were climbing up the stairs and going inside. Most of them were wearing bags on their backs or carrying bags with wheels—the kind Revver had seen at the airport.

The human in uniform yelled out, "Eight fifteen to Charlotte! All aboard!" The bell rang again.

"I need to get on. How do I do it?"

Hisssssss! The train sounded out again.

"I have absolutely no idea."

"Wait, wh-wh-what do you mean?"

"Revver, I've learned many things from observing. I've had lessons from my journeys and from listening to other birds. But as you might suspect, none of us has ever needed to board a train."

This made sense, of course. But Revver had gotten so used to relying on Blue. It was scary to think he'd have to figure this out on his own.

"I suspect you need to go up those stairs. Unless you have a better idea."

Revver nodded. It did seem like the only way.

"Well, go ahead, then; I'm going to head back to Median before it gets too much later. It's been a long day."

"Yes. It has. Okay, well, um, goodbye."

"Goodbye, Revver. And good luck to you."

"Thank you, Blue. I'll never forget this."

"Happy to *take you under my wing*, Revver!" Blue chuckled. "Ha-ha! Just a little bird humor there!" he said.

Revver looked blank.

"Hmph! No one seems to get my jokes," Blue mumbled as he started to flap his wings to fly.

"Wait. Please. Um. Um, just one last question."

"Of course."

"Why?"

"Why *what*?"

"Why did you help me?"

"Hmm," Blue hummed. "I don't understand the question."

"You—and Glee and Chipmunk—did *so much* for me. And *you've* been helping me the entire day. I'm sure you had better things to do."

"I had other things to do. Not *better* things."

"But why . . ."

"Revver, why did YOU help that driver back there? You *certainly* had other things to do."

Revver said nothing. Actually, he wasn't sure why.

"Because, Revver, KINDNESS. It's given out and passed around until it makes a big circle. Kindness gives way to kindness."

The circle! Revver thought. Finally, he understood! *It's all connected!* **Everything really IS connected to everything else!** The more he experienced, the more he learned, the more this proved to be true.

"Will you please tell Glee and Chipmunk that I made it this far?"

"Certainly. But I hope to give them the news that you made it safely to the speedway."

"How will you *know* if I make it?"

"Because, Revver, birds know everything."

33

He waited until the uniform-wearing human turned away, went up the stairs, and disappeared into the train. Then Revver jumped up the stairs and scurried inside, just as the door closed behind him. He wasn't sure if squirrels were welcome on the train, and he couldn't risk being kicked off. So he pressed himself against the closed door and sunk down low, hoping no one would see him in the dim light.

He was in a little room. Ahead of him was another closed door.

On his left and his right were other doors. He guessed that those doors led to the train cars and that he was someplace in between.

The train hissed again. He felt the train lurch and start to roll. He could hear the wheels *thud-thud . . . thud-thud*. It felt like the train was picking up speed. Going *fast* always made him feel excited.

He heard a loudspeaker. "Welcome, passengers, to the eight fifteen nonstop to Charlotte. I'll be coming to collect tickets. Please sit back, relax, and enjoy your ride this evening."

Another human in a uniform opened the door on Revver's right side. Revver sunk down lower. The human sniffed and mumbled, "Smells terrible in here." But she walked straight through to the other side. When that door opened, the human called out, "Tickets, please! Please have your tickets ready." Then she disappeared into the other car.

Revver looked down at himself, and he almost didn't recognize what he saw. His fur was matted, stiff, and filthy. He caught a look at himself in the shiny metal door in front of him and gasped. He was an absolute mess.

The rhythm of the train was comforting, *thud-thud . . . thud-thud.* For the first time since he opened his eyes this morning, Revver took a deep breath. He noticed he felt cold. He slumped back against the metal door again and made himself into a very tight ball. He thought back on the day. He realized how tired and sore he was.

I should rest a little. Tomorrow will be another long day. Revver closed his eyes and allowed himself to relax. He sniffled. He sneezed. He tried to curl up into a tighter ball to keep himself warm, but he still shivered.

34

The brakes squealed as the train slowed. The sound startled Revver, and he was suddenly alert. He crouched near the door, waiting to see what would happen next.

Then Revver heard the loudspeaker. "Folks, we're just about to arrive in Charlotte, our final destination. Thank you for traveling with us tonight. Please make sure to take all your things with you."

The human in the uniform came into the little room, and Revver held his breath. But the human did not look Revver's way. Instead, she turned away, standing with her back to Revver, facing the opposite door.

As the train came to a stop, people started coming into the little room from the cars on the left and the right, carrying their bags and boxes. They all had their backs to Revver, waiting for the door opposite him to open. Revver felt relief that they weren't facing *his* door, or he would surely be seen.

As the humans crowded in, Revver heard someone whisper, "Ugh, it smells awful in here."

A small human said loudly, "Mama, it's smelly!"

Revver was nose-blind to himself. But he guessed, *I must **really** stink.*

When the last humans filed out the door and down the step, Revver seized the chance. He ran out—fast. He heard someone squeal as he went by, "What **was** that?!" But Revver was quickly gone and out of sight.

It was the middle of the night. Revver stopped and thought for a few moments. He sniffled and sneezed again. *I should have a plan. How am I going to find the track?* But for the life of him, he could not think of anything; his brain felt heavy and foggy. It was a warm night, but he still felt cold. He decided that some sleep would be the best idea; he'd figure out a plan in the morning.

It was so dark that Revver had a hard time finding his way. He walked a long while. Finally, with the help of a small sliver of moonlight, he found a tree. He had no idea what was around him, but he climbed up. He came upon a large branch with a crease in it. He squeezed in, and it was comfortable and perfect.

He started to think. *Just one night ago, I was in Median. The night before that, I was at the airport . . .* Or was he? He tried to put things together. He had lost track of how many days had passed. He needed to know! *I have to figure out how much time I have before race day, before the team leaves Charlotte!* But his thoughts were all jumbled up. Now he felt so cold that he was shivering. His head hurt. Actually, *everything* hurt. He'd been banged up in the journey—his face, his paws, his tummy—but this was a deeper hurting than that. It hurt to lift his arm or his head. He hurt INSIDE.

Even his tail felt achy. He felt dizzy. It was very different than the two-pink-doughnuts feeling. But even through the fog in his head, he knew something was wrong.

Revver was sick.

35

Revver slept and slept. He dreamed jumbled dreams. He dreamed of his squirrel family and his racing family, all together. He dreamed about Bill. He dreamed about pooping in the garage. He dreamed of Blue and Glee and Chipmunk. He thought about the crate and Median and flying off the spinning tower of sunglasses. He dreamed about the delicious cold drops he'd tasted in the airport and smacked his lips in his sleep.

He had nightmares about coyotes and hawks and snakes and cars squealing onto the shoulder of the highway, all too close for him to run away. He dreamed about driving the white toilet machines on the track at full speed, with the screaming human chasing him. But in his dreams, the screaming human turned into *Jack!* He dreamed about the flat *something* in the road; he looked at the something more closely and saw . . . *himself!* Then he dreamed about Lou and groaned out, loud and angry.

A thoughtful cardinal brought some berries and nuts and left them beside him. Revver looked at the cardinal with half-closed eyes and nodded, as best as he could nod, to say thank you. He nibbled lightly at the snacks and then fell back to sleep. *Kindness*, Revver thought peacefully.

Revver reached down to his ankle, to touch the chain that Sprite had made for him. In his dreams, it was still there, and Revver sighed, relieved.

Sometimes, a feeling of panic would run through him and he would remember: *The track! I have to get to the track! I'm running out of time! They will leave without me!* He would lift his aching head and try to move, but it felt so heavy and awful that all he could do was put it down and fall back to sleep.

A bluebird came and kept him company for a while. The bird stayed beside him as he slept, but Revver was not sure if the bird was real or a dream.

The sun rose and set. Sometimes, there was rain. Revver barely noticed.

Revver's eyes popped open, wide, and he looked around. It was morning. He wasn't sure how long he had slept. He breathed in a deep breath of fresh air and took stock of himself: he felt better! It took him a moment to remember where he was—and why.

I'm in Charlotte! I need to get to the track! **Now, how do I find the track?!** Revver had no better idea than to just start *moving*. He scurried down the tree.

Above him, birds watched.

Soon, Revver found himself on a tree-lined street with houses on either side. The trees shaded him from the hot sun, and Revver walked in the thick grass to keep his paws cool. The very few cars that passed by were traveling nice and slowly. He could smell freshly cut grass. He could hear small humans making happy sounds, laughing and squealing. *This seems like a nice place to be,* Revver thought as he strolled along.

Then Revver heard a sound that was NOT happy. He walked toward the sound, ahead of him. It sounded like a high-pitched scream. Revver could hear fluttering. As he came upon the scream, "Help! Help! Help me!" Revver looked up. On the top floor of a house, a bird was flailing on a windowsill, flapping its wings, trying to get loose. From the ground, Revver could not see *why* the bird was stuck. But he could see that the bird was bright red—*a cardinal!* Revver sprang into action.

He made his way up the house quickly, first climbing a trellis, then jumping from the trellis to the tree, onto a gutter pipe, to a piece of wooden trim, and, at last, to the windowsill.

But he still could not quite understand what was happening. He went closer. The bird was on its side with its legs straight out, kicking furiously and flapping its wings. The bird's high-pitched shriek was unbearable! A few red feathers floated around.

When Revver inched closer, he could see that the window was open, just a crack, at the bottom. *Just enough* for a paw, with its sharp claws drawn, to hold down the struggling bird. Neither the bird nor the owner of the claw saw Revver. But the sight of the poor, screaming bird was too much! Revver roared, ***"Vr-vr-vr-VRRROOOOM!"*** as he sprang. The paw loosened its grip. Revver easily lifted up the paw to free the bird.

The bird struggled a little to get back onto its feet. Then it flew up to the top of the window frame . . . and watched.

Revver held the paw tightly with *both* his paws. He used his own claws for extra security.

Revver looked down at the paw. It was white and fluffy. Revver looked into the window, furious at whoever would hurt the poor red bird. He glared at the animal on the other side of the window—and *gasped!* Pressed against the glass, Revver saw: **Lou!**

Revver remembered what Glee had said about FATE. Was it FATE that brought him here, to Lou, so that he could get his bracelet back?!

"What *are* you?! What do you *want* with me?!"

Revver's thoughts were speeding by. He was excited but confused. So he said nothing and tried to collect himself. *Did Lou ask,* What *are* you?! *How odd! I'm a squirrel! He knows darn well what I am!* Revver just glared at Lou. Remembering what Lou had done, seeing him try to hurt the cardinal, Revver wasn't sure he'd ever felt so angry in his life! He blared out again, even more loudly, *"Vr-vr-vr-VR-RROOOOM!"* and he pulled the paw harder out of the window. Now the cat's face was smashed up against the glass, and the cat looked scared.

"Wh-wh-what . . . **WHAT. ARE. YOU?!** What do you want with me?!"

Then Revver caught a split-second glimpse of his own reflection in the window. First, he was shocked at how he looked—even worse than on the train! Then it almost made him laugh. Revver looked HORRIFYING. *No wonder* Lou kept asking what he was! Revver did NOT look at all like a squirrel but more like some kind of matted, long-tailed swamp monster—that roared!

"NEVER!" Revver yelled. "You will NEVER touch a bird again, EVER!"

"Um, um, um . . . well, okay, then. Thank you. Now *I'm sure* you must be going."

Revver pulled harder on Lou's paw, and Lou was even more smashed up against the window. Lou looked like a flattened marshmallow!

"Fine! Fine! OKAY! FINE! I'll NEVER touch a bird again! I promise!"

Revver felt a moment of being in control. He felt powerful! He decided to throw in another demand. "OR a chipmunk! You cannot touch a chipmunk, either!"

For a moment, Lou had forgotten to be scared. He was insulted! "Now, *why*? That's just *rrrrr*-ridiculous! Why not a chipmunk? They're so tasty, and they're such awful, pesky *rrr*-roden—"

"STOP!" Revver growled. The word "rodent" made Revver angrier. The thought of someone eating his friend Chipmunk made him EVEN ANGRIER than that! He roared again, one of his loudest, most ferocious roars *ever*, *"Vr-vr-vr-VRR-ROOOOM!"* and he tugged on Lou's paw, wrist, and now his entire arm.

"Okay! **FINE!** You win! No chipmunks, either! Jeez! How's a *purrr*-fect, *domesticated* creature like *me* supposed to amuse myself?"

Revver growled, remembering the airport. **"What about all those *interesting ideas* that keep your brain busy?"**

Lou looked stunned to hear his own words back at him.

Revver pulled harder.

"FINE! OKAY!!! I SAID: **I. AGREE!**"

"I. WILL. KNOW. I **will** come back."

"N-n-n-no. You won't need to come back. I promise! No more birds. No chipmunks. Fine!"

"One more thing," Revver said, trying to use his scariest voice. "I'm going to let you have your

arm back. I've decided NOT to squeeze you out through the crack under this window, bit by bit, and . . ."
Hmm, Revver thought . . . *what should I say next?* He raised his voice even louder. **"And I'm not going to . . . *EAT YOU!*"**

"**Eat me?!?!?!** No! I mean, yes! I mean, that's DEFINITELY the right decision! I'm sure I'd taste terrible. I mean, look at me, I'm all fur! Well, thick, gorgeous fur, *of course*, but fur nonetheless." Lou laughed—a scared, uncomfortable, not-really-laughing laugh.

"But in exchange for NOT eating you, I'm going to need some kind of *payment*—for providing the service of NOT eating you."

"Payment, uh, uh, uh, of course . . . Um, let me think, um, uh . . . did you have something in mind?"

"A cord. An orange chain, made of braided stems."

"Well, um, well . . ." Lou laughed uneasily. "Um, that is QUITE specific . . ."

Revver growled and pressed his face to the glass, staring Lou in the eyes. He pulled harder on Lou's arm.

"Um, well, I'll tell you . . . and you'll find this to be QUITE a coincidence, but a *pathetic rodent* DID give me something like that just a few days ago . . ."

"Hand. It. Over."

"Well, but, but, here's the thing . . . and I'm, I'm sure you'll find this humorous . . . it was a pittance of a trinket, really. Quite nasty. No value, I'm *certain*. I looked at it for a few moments, but it was not worth my time. I discarded it."

"You . . . DISCARDED IT?!?!"

"Yes, well, that is to say that I, well, I *threw it away*. Tossed it onto the floor. Ditched it! Dismissed it! However you would like to phrase it, **I got rid of that DISGUSTING thing**. But wait! Just *look at me*! Look at *this collar*!" Lou tilted his head to show off a shiny black collar with big, sparkly rocks on it. "It's ALMOST as *purr*-fect and dazzling as I am! How about if you take THIS for payment? It's worth *so much more* than that scrap of orange garbage anyway!"

Revver could feel the vein in his forehead pulsing, just like Jack's. He had a sudden urge to pounce on Lou and bite him right in the face!

That's another problem with windows! Revver was on one side, and Lou was on the other.

Revver waited a long time, pulling harder and harder on Lou's arm until he could get his thoughts together. Lou still looked terrified.

Revver pulled just a bit harder and smooshed Lou's face even more against the glass. "You are DONE being . . ." Revver fumbled to find the right word. "A BULLY!"

"Yes, yes! YES! Of course! For sure! I promise!"

Finally Revver exhaled. He snarled, "Just remember my warning . . . **Lou!!!**"

Revver's face was pressed against one side of the glass. Lou's face was smashed against the other. They stared eye to eye. And suddenly, Lou's mind *flashed*! He had seen those eyes before! He gasped. Now Lou KNEW who was holding him!

"But, but, but . . . h-h-how? H-h-how did you find me?"

Revver growled and roared one final time, and he let go of Lou.

Lou quickly ran away from the window. He disappeared deep inside the house, sobbing *meow-meow-meow* the entire way.

Revver climbed back down to the ground. *I was SO CLOSE to getting the chain back.* He was so disappointed and sad.

FATE had led him to Lou, and then FATE had let him down.

36

Revver started back on his way, returning to the route where he had left off.

"Wait! Woo-hoo-*wait*!" The cardinal was fluttering, flying over Revver's shoulder.

Revver didn't pay much attention. He was too deep in his own thoughts, worrying about getting to the track.

"Thank you."

"You're welcome." Revver continued trudging.

"But wait . . . Why did you help me?"

"Well, why not?"

"I'm sure you had better things to do!"

Revver thought about Blue. "I had **other** things to do. Not **better** things."

Revver paused, then added, "Why did YOU help ME, when I was sick in the tree? That was you, wasn't it?"

"Well, you know."

"Kindness," they both said together.

The bird flew alongside him, but Revver barely noticed. He kept walking. Once again, he had time to make up.

"Um, may I ask you . . . REVVER, right?"

Now Revver stopped. "How do you know my name?"

"Word gets around."

Revver said nothing but peered up into the trees. The trees were filled with . . . birds. All of them were watching.

"Thank you again for the help back there."

"Why were you so close to him? Aren't birds supposed to know *everything*? You MUST KNOW that he's horrible."

"Well, *of course* I know. I got my house numbers mixed up. There's a canary in a house on this block who I heard needed some company."

"Oh."

"You don't look like I expected. I mean, um, well, you don't look like the squirrels I've seen before."

"It's been a hard trip."

"I can smell that. I mean, SEE! I meant, **SEE THAT.**"

Revver sighed. He started walking.

"My name is Charlotte."

Revver stopped again. "Your NAME is *Charlotte?* And you LIVE in *Charlotte?*"

"Yes, well, I have three older siblings, all named Cardinal. My mother decided to get creative."

Revver thought this was odd, but he said nothing. He had begun walking again when he got an idea: *Birds know* **everything**, he thought.

He turned to the cardinal. "Charlotte, do you know what day it is? I've lost track. I've been traveling, and then I was sick, and I don't know how long *that* was . . . and so now, I need to know what day it is, because practice is on Friday, and qualifying's on Saturday, and the race is on Sunday, and then the team leaves for the next track . . ."

"Today is Sunday."

Revver looked at the ground. This was the worst news.

"But it's early! You still have time!"

Revver felt hopeless . . . getting to the track felt like such a huge feat.

"Revver?"

"Yes?"

"Would you like me to lead you to the track?"

37

A few raindrops started to fall as they continued on, just a drop here and a drop there—*at first*. But after a while, the rain grew steadier. Revver kept trudging through, for a long time. But now it was pouring—so fast and hard that they could barely see. Charlotte could not fly through the downpour. Revver was heavy and soaked. They needed to stop.

They found their way under a porch to wait out the storm.

"I hate rain."

"You do? I like it. It gets everything so fresh and clean. And, Revver, think of where we'd be

without rain: no water for us, no water for the trees and plants that give us food . . ."

"It just always seems to come at the wrong time."

"Hmm . . ."

Silence.

"I don't like windows," Charlotte offered.

"Me either! I bump into them ALL THE TIME!"

"I've flown into quite a few. It's so irritating! I just don't see them sometimes."

"Exactly!"

They both laughed. Revver felt like he had another friend.

"Charlotte, do you know what *domesticated* is?"

"Yes. Why do you ask?"

"Someone once told me I *wasn't* domesticated."

"Well, it means that you have lived with humans your whole life."

Revver thought about this. He realized that Lou was right. "Oh," he said, a little disappointed.

"But, Revver . . ."

"Yes?"

"Being *domesticated* doesn't make you *good*. Just like NOT being domesticated doesn't make you bad. The most important thing is how we treat each other, not where we come from.

"Does that make sense?"

"I guess so?"

"Someone who would say something *just* to hurt your feelings is NOT kind. That Lou is mean and awful, and being *domesticated* doesn't change that."

"Wait, how did you know it was . . . ? Oh. Never mind."

"You're good. You're kind. That's what matters!"

"But, Charlotte, am I . . . *a rodent?*"

"Does that word hurt your feelings?"

"I . . . I think so."

Charlotte was quiet for a while.

"Basically," Charlotte continued, "a *rodent* is just a furry animal who nibbles."

"Oh! Well, that doesn't sound so bad!"

"Plus!" Now Charlotte sounded excited. "Forty percent—*that's almost HALF!*—of all the mammals *in the whole wide world* are **rodents**! There are rodents on EVERY CONTINENT—well, except Antarctica. Did you know that?!"

"No."

"It's TRUE! Forty percent, Revver! That's a LOT!"

"Wow!" Revver did not understand most of what Charlotte said. He definitely didn't know what a percent was—or a continent or Antarctica. Or how a cardinal would know such things. But he *definitely* understood that there were A LOT of creatures just. Like. Him.

"But, Revver, some people say *rodent* to mean *pest*. Like, something annoying that they'd want to get rid of."

"Oh." Revver considered this. It didn't feel very good.

"So, Revver, while you are technically a *rodent*, you are certainly NOT a *pest*."

Revver was quiet for a while. "I've learned that birds know things, but I didn't realize that they know SO much."

"Really? Haven't you ever heard someone say, 'A little birdie told me . . .'?"

"No, I've never heard that."

"It's a phrase, you know. It's said *a lot*."

"Said a lot by *whom?*"

"Everyone."

Revver decided, "Maybe it just hasn't caught on with squirrels."

38

Revver was thinking, *It's* Sunday. *It's getting later and later. I'm not going to get there in time.*

Finally, the rain slowed enough for them to start on their way again. Charlotte flew up and ahead, the same way Blue had done. Revver wondered if this was just something else birds knew: how to lead squirrels where they needed to go.

The sun peeked out, and a light wind was blowing. They were finally drying off.

"Not much farther," Charlotte encouraged.

"I'm afraid I'm going to miss it."

"I can fly faster."

"No, I mean, we've lost most of the day. They're going to leave without me."

"Stay hopeful, Revver. Maybe they'll be delayed."

Charlotte sped up a bit. Revver picked up his pace. But thinking about the team being *delayed* fired something in his mind. "Charlotte!!! Wait!!!"

She hovered overhead, waiting.

"DELAYED! They'll be delayed! It's been raining!!! They don't race in the rain! They WILL be delayed!!! A RAIN DELAY!!!"

"Well, if that's the case, then they're *very* delayed. It rained most of yesterday, too."

"It did?" The past few days, when he was sick, were a blur . . .

"It did."

"That's GREAT NEWS, Charlotte! Thank you! THANK YOU!!!" Revver looked up at the sky. "You bought me time! Thank you, rain! I love you, rain!"

Charlotte laughed. "I guess it rained at the *right time* for you this time." She glanced back at Revver and GASPED!

It scared Revver. "What?! What is it?! What's wrong?!"

"Revver! You! You . . . you . . . you . . . you look . . . LIKE A SQUIRREL!" She flew down near him. "And . . . you don't stink!"

"I'm . . . *clean?*" There was a car parked just ahead of them by the curb. Revver ran over and looked at his reflection in the hubcap. "Charlotte! Look at me! I'm clean!"

"You just needed a nice, long shower! I told you—rain is good! You're all fresh and clean!"

They both laughed. Revver felt giddy. It was the best he could remember feeling in a very, very long time. The team was still here! He was clean! He was jumping and twirling! He was looking at the sky. "Thank you, rain! Thank you for the shower! Thank you for the rain delay!" Revver jumped for joy.

SCREEEeeeeeeeCH! Revver heard the sound. He heard Charlotte screaming his name. He turned to look. He only had time to jump.

And then Revver was hit by a car.

39

He was flat on his belly—again. He checked himself before he opened his eyes. He took the hit with his chest and his face. They stung, but not terribly. His arm hurt a little, too. He tried to wiggle it. It seemed to move the right way. Revver took a breath. *I'm alive. I'm not flat*, he thought.

He opened his eyes. The car was stopped, and Revver's face was pressed against the windshield. He righted himself and looked in at the horrified face of the driver.

Through the windshield, Revver stared at the driver's face. Now the driver looked shocked instead of horrified. Revver looked closer and sat up taller.

Now the driver had the biggest smile Revver had ever seen—the big, broad smile of a driver on the winners' podium. The smiling was confusing for Revver. *Why would a driver be smiling after he crashed into a squirrel?*

Suddenly, the driver made Revver forget how much he didn't like windows. This was *the best, most wonderful, most amazing window* in the entire world!

The driver opened his car door and jumped out. He instantly grabbed Revver off the windshield and hugged him tightly, sobbing.

Revver decided that Glee was probably right about FATE after all.

The driver was Bill.

40

Bill did not stop hugging Revver for a long time. He kept saying, "I can't believe I found you! Is it really *you?*"

Then Revver would nod, as best as a squirrel can nod, and Bill would laugh and hug Revver tighter.

Charlotte flew by and landed on a nearby tree. "WOW, Revver! WOW! That was a **close** one! You are ONE. LUCKY. SQUIRREL."

Bill kept talking. "How *on earth* did you find Charlotte?!" Bill didn't really expect an answer, since, of course, he did not speak Squirrel.

"Wait!!!" Charlotte was startled. "How does he know my name?!"

"He means Charlotte *the place*. Not Charlotte *the who*—I mean, *the you*."

"Oh. Wow. That's very confusing."

"Tell me about it." Revver tipped his head toward Bill. "Charlotte, this is Bill. Bill is part of my racing fam—"

"I know all about Bill." Charlotte cut him off.

Revver nodded. *Of course she does*, he thought.

"It was nice meeting you, Revver. Thank you again for saving me from that *awful* cat."

"Thank you for leading the way here."

Charlotte nodded, chirped, and began to flap her wings.

"Wait. Charlotte . . . ?"

"Yes?"

"This has been a pretty exciting day, hasn't it? I mean, with Lou and then me getting hit by the car . . ."

"It's been the MOST exciting day EVER! It's been a wonderful, exciting day!"

"Well, would you mind . . . I mean, I have some friends who I think would like to know that I'm here. And those friends—they helped me, and they LOVE exciting stories, and . . ."

"I know, Revver."

"Oh. Okay."

"Don't worry, Revver. They'll hear all about this!"

"Thank you, Charlotte."

Charlotte was just about to go. "Oh, and Revver . . ."

"What?"

"Stay in your crate next time. You *really* have to try to **Be More Patient.**"

Revver nodded. He watched Charlotte fly away. *'Bye, Charlotte*, he thought.

Bill stopped hugging Revver. Bill's eyes were still wet and red, but he was smiling a huge smile. He walked around and set Revver onto the front seat of the car, right on top of a nice, fluffy shop towel. Revver snuggled in. It felt better than he remembered.

"I just can't believe I really found you!" Bill looked at Revver, concerned. "You feelin' okay? Are you okay, bud?" Bill was rubbing Revver's head.

215

Revver nodded—his best nod.

"Okay. I hope so. You got rattled around pretty good back there.

"Oh! Hang on." Bill reached into his pocket and poured some nuts out for Revver. Revver nibbled a few.

"You up for headin' to the track?"

Revver popped up onto his back feet. **"Vr-vr-vr-VRRROOOOM!"**

It made Bill jump, and he threw his head back and laughed. "Well, that's good, because I know a few folks who are gonna be awful happy to see you."

Bill got into the driver's side. The car started moving.

"Revver, I gotta tell you, I've been looking EVERYWHERE for ya. When I saw your crate was empty, I missed the flight to look for ya. I musta spent ten hours wanderin' around that dang airport tryin' to find you. Boy, I was scared." Bill paused and looked at Revver. Revver felt awful thinking about Bill being scared. Revver knew what that felt like.

"And then I got a car so I could drive around and keep looking. The team told me there was no use, but somethin' just told me to keep lookin'."

Maybe a bird?! Revver thought.

"Finally, I just had to leave. I couldn't stay back any longer. I had to get here for the race."

Revver nodded. He understood.

They drove in silence. Revver watched out the window.

"Oh! Hey! Wait." Bill held the steering wheel with his left hand while he fumbled through his pocket. "Hang on . . . I know it's in here . . ."

Revver hoped it was NOT a piece of doughnut.

"Hey! Here it is!"

Bill put something on the seat beside Revver. "I found this on the floor after the plane left. I thought you might want it back."

It was the chain that Sprite had made for him.

41

They arrived at the track and went through the gate. They got to the garage, and Bill parked next to the car hauler.

Bill was talking on his phone as he carried Revver into the garage. Revver was SO EXCITED to see everyone, he was almost holding his breath. But no one was inside.

Bill turned to Revver. "Now, bud, I know you're not gonna like this, but I think you should stay here and relax awhile. You took a good hit back there. The car's heading over to the tech tent for inspection. I'm gonna run down there and see what's up. You can wander to the pit once the race starts."

Revver nodded. He knew about inspection. If there was anything wrong with the car or if things weren't *exactly* right, they could not race. Tech was a big deal. It made everyone nervous.

Revver didn't mind sitting in the garage for a little while; he wanted to sit and think about everything that had happened—so many things, so quickly. He thought about everyone who had helped him along the way. He decided that he'd sort of had his *own* team to help him get to his *own* finish line—here. He might never see them again, but he knew they were out there. Even though that felt a little sad, it also felt okay. He also realized that he had only come across ONE awful Lou but FOUR awesome others who had helped him. He decided that that meant that the world was more good than bad.

Revver remembered what Joe had said to him. *I'll tell ya—it's a big, big world out there, and you're a little guy* . . . Revver now knew that was true. But the world was *less* big with help along the way. Revver decided this needed to be a note for his brain burrow, but he could not figure out how to say it. Finally, he decided: Be Kind.

Now he sat and enjoyed the sounds of the track—all the excitement of the fans before the race. The familiar smells. He was so happy to be back.

Then Revver heard a different sound: *Crrrrr.* He heard a voice say, "Do you copy?"

He looked around, but he didn't see anyone.

He heard, *Crrrrr.* He waited and listened. Then he heard a different voice. "Casey. This is Jack. Can you hear me? Over."

This was confusing. Casey was the driver. Jack, the team owner, was talking to the driver. But why was Revver hearing that, here, in the garage?

Crrrr-crrr. Now another voice, the crew chief, said, "Casey, we got about two seconds to get through tech. They're about to disqualify us. We need to hear from you. Over."

Then Revver heard Jack's loudest, scariest voice. "Casey! Dagnabbit! ANSWER US!"

In a split second, Revver realized what was

happening: **THE RADIO! The car's radio had been left behind!** The car HAD to have a radio. The driver HAD to be able to communicate with his crew chief and his spotter. Without the radio, the car would not pass inspection, and they would not be racing.

Revver started to look around, frantic. He ran and dug and shuffled things around. Finally, he spied it on top of the counter, under a package of batteries. *Here! Here it is!* He grabbed it. He held it above his head and started  running like his life depended on it.

He darted through fans and between car haulers and people with cameras and microphones. He had never been to this track before, so he was trying hard to figure out his way to the inspection area. He darted one way and then the other, avoiding feet at every turn. He was going FAST—SO MUCH FASTER than any human could have run.

Finally, he saw their team car, near the tent. He could hear Jack yelling. He could see Bill and some of the other team members pacing. He could see track officials walking around and measuring the car.

"Vr-vr-vr-VRRROOOOM!" Revver roared out.

Everyone looked up at the same time as Revver ran in. Revver ran through SO MANY people, all looking at him. Someone holding a big camera followed Revver to the car. Revver ran to Bill, who took the radio and handed it to Casey.

Jack looked to the sky, the same way Revver did when he'd thanked the rain clouds. The rest of the team applauded. Bill picked up Revver and rubbed him behind the ears, and then everyone wanted to pat Revver. Revver looked over and saw an official nod and give a "thumbs-up."

They could race.

42

It was a long, hard race. There were crashes. Some cars had trouble with tires, others with engines. A lot of cars did not finish or had big setbacks.

But at the end of the day, Casey won.

As their car crossed the finish line, the team exploded in the pits, hugging and high-fiving and cheering. Everyone was so happy! Revver looked above and saw Jack, standing on the pit wagon, smiling and holding his fists in the air in victory. He was shaking lots of hands and getting lots of pats on his back.

Revver felt good that Jack was happy.

Casey rolled through the pits and lowered his window net to high-five and shake hands with the team. Bill held up Revver. "Glad to have you back," Casey yelled above the noise, as he high-fived Revver's paw.

Bill and Casey met eyes. Bill tilted his head toward Revver. Casey nodded and said, "Revver, do you feel like takin' a little victory ride with me?"

Seriously? Revver was in disbelief. *I do! Of course! **Of course I do!*** He quickly nodded—as best as a squirrel can nod!

Bill handed Revver to Casey. Revver jumped far back in the car so he could brace himself. Casey sped back onto the track. Revver held on TIGHT.

The speed was AMAZING! The sound vibrated right through him! *This is the best, the best,* **THE BEST!**

Casey drove toward the start-finish line and began revving the engine and spinning the tires. It felt WILD! Revver could *feel* the engine roaring; he could smell the burning rubber. He could see the smoking tires. In the background, he could hear Casey's name on the loudspeaker. He could hear the crowd cheering. Revver ROARED right along with the crowd and the car, *"Vr-vr-vr-VRRROOOOOOOOOOOOOM!"*

Casey took a quick look back at Revver and laughed. Then he hit the gas. The car lurched forward so hard, Revver felt like he was glued to the back of the car, and *he loved it.*

"Do ya feel like a few doughnuts?" Casey asked, laughing.

Doughnuts?! The idea was awful. Revver could not even THINK of eating a doughnut, ESPECIALLY at a time like this!

Then Casey started spinning the car—fast. The car went around and around and around and around. "Woo-hoo!" Casey screamed. "Nothin' tastes better than *victory doughnuts*, right, Revver?!"

Doughnuts? THIS is doughnuts, too?! Just like the other doughnuts, this kind gave Revver an upset tummy! But Casey soon straightened the car and Revver felt better—GREAT, in fact. An official handed Casey the checkered flag, and Casey did a few more burnouts, spinning the wheels of the car until it was so smoky that Revver could not see a thing. The crowd was still cheering.

Casey carried Revver toward the podium. Lots of humans took their picture as Casey climbed up to the highest step.

But Revver jumped to Bill. Revver tried to hide under Bill's arm, so Bill held Revver close and covered him with a hat. Revver *knew* what came next: the winners were going to splash fizzing liquid all over each other and the crew. Revver had been wet and filthy enough for a while. He was finally clean. Maybe being sprayed would be fun another time—but NOT today.

43

"Another race, another place," Bill said as the crew gathered in the garage to pack up.

Joe picked up Revver and greeted him with a big hug before he started loading the cars into the hauler. "I thought we'd lost you, fella. Glad to have you back," Joe whispered to him.

Revver nodded—to show Joe that he was glad to be back, too.

Revver put away tools and helped to pack up. He scurried around and checked insides and outsides of things to make sure they had everything and everything was in its place. Sometimes Revver could spot things that the others missed.

He was small enough to squeeze into and under places that the humans couldn't. There *were* advantages to being the only squirrel on the team. And, it turned out, there were advantages to *having* the only squirrel on a team.

When Revver looked up, he noticed that everyone was standing around him, staring at him. It was strange.

"Hey, Revver," Susan said, and she kneeled down to Revver, "*a little birdie told us* that you might like these."

Who? Revver wondered. *Blue? Charlotte? The sparrow from the airport? Someone else?* He looked around at everyone. Joe and Bill were smiling the biggest.

Susan held a box toward Revver. She took off the lid so that Revver could see: *a perfectly Revver-size pair of* **sparkly blue sunglasses**!

Susan helped Revver put them on. "You look awesome, Revver," she said, patting his head and standing around with the others. Revver looked at everyone. Everyone looked at Revver.

Revver blasted out his approval. *"Vr-vr-vr-VRRROOOOM!"*

"Now what's going on here?!" Jack had burst in and saw the team standing around. Everyone was quiet. Then Jack saw Revver. Revver was nervous.

Jack was standing with another human, who was wearing a large hat. They walked right to Revver. "Well, now! *Here's* our man of the hour!" Jack said, pointing down toward Revver so the human with the hat could see him. Jack was smiling. Revver thought it was weird to see Jack smile so much in one day.

The human with the hat knelt down to Revver. Revver could tell that the man felt awkward. He probably didn't talk to squirrels very much.

"Um, well, howdy there, little guy." The human put out his hand, and Revver held up his paw for a handshake. "So I've been hearing an awful lot about you and, see, I'd like to, well, *sponsor you*. What do ya think about that?" Then the human laughed. "Well, not YOU, of course; I mean *the team*."

The human stood up and spoke to everyone. "Y'all, I own The Delight Company—you know, we make healthy food for all different animals. I'm sure you've seen it: Horse Delight and Rabbit Delight and Chicken Delight and Cat Delight . . ."

Revver shuddered at the thought of cats.

The man went on. "And, of course, *Squirrel Delight!*"

Revver heard someone say, "Really?"

"So *of course*, I can't think of a more PERFECT way to advertise than with your team, on your car. Now, Jack and I are still working out the details, but I like to think that, before the end of the season, your car will be decorated with a picture of Revver next to a big bag of *Squirrel Delight!*"

Everyone seemed excited to hear this.

Revver guessed that this was good news. He really did not understand anything about *sponsorship*. But his team was happy, so he was happy. And he was pretty sure that this meant he was NOT *out*.

44

It felt like packing up was taking a very long time. Revver didn't care. He was being *more patient.* And he was just happy to be with his family.

At last, Bill brought out the crate. "Sorry, bud," Bill said, "we need to try this again. I'll double-check that I lock it this time."

Revver jumped right in and snuggled into the towel. He reached down and felt the chain around his ankle. It reminded him of his grove family. He smiled. He just *knew* he'd see them again sometime, because, FATE. Or maybe birds would be involved somehow? He wasn't *exactly* sure **how,** but he was definitely sure.

They got into a car, then walked through a new airport. They took a shuttle train. They went on moving steps and moving floors. They boarded an airplane and sped down the runway and *zoomed!* up into the sky. They landed and walked through another airport and took another shuttle train and got into another car. It was SUCH an exciting day, with SO MANY exciting things to see!

But Revver would have to find that out on their *next* trip, because he slept the entire way.

He had had enough excitement for a while anyway. Today, he didn't care where, how, or how fast they went.

He was with Bill, so he was already home.